CW01646428

FIRE AT WILL

The 8.8 opened up. [illegible] cracked out.
The lance of flame, vivid in the dusk, pointed directly at the target.
The concussion boomed and bellowed.
Wolz looked across.
That would wake them up!
Where the shot went he had no idea.
The gun crew slammed the breech open, the next round slammed in, the breech closed, the men waited as the layer took careful aim, and then – *blam*! Quite clearly, on the black hull of the ship, a rose of flame jetted before instantly disappearing. Smoke lifted.
A hit.

Also by Bruno Krauss in Sphere Books:

SEA WOLF: STEEL SHARK
SEA WOLF: SHARK NORTH
SEA WOLF: SHARK PACK
SEA WOLF: SHARK HUNT
SEA WOLF: SHARK AFRICA
SEA WOLF: SHARK RAID
SEA WOLF: SHARK AMERICA

Sea Wolf: Shark Trap

BRUNO KRAUSS

SPHERE BOOKS LIMITED
30-32 Gray's Inn Road, London WC1X 8JL

First published in Great Britain by
Sphere Books Ltd 1982
Copyright © Bruno Krauss 1982

TRADE
MARK

This book is sold subject to the condition that it shall not, by way of trade or otherwise, be lent, re-sold, hired out or otherwise circulated without the publisher's prior consent in any form of binding or cover other than that in which it it published and without a similar condition including this condition being imposed on the subsequent purchaser.

Set in Plantin

Printed and bound in Great Britain by
Hunt Barnard Printing Ltd, Aylesbury, Bucks.

1

The wasserbomben seized U-451 in their jaws and shook her until her rivets rattled. The pattern of charges dropped by the US destroyer fell to starboard and a fraction high. Only a few metres separated U-451 from total destruction.

Kapitänleutnant Baldur Wolz gripped onto the chart table and hauled himself off the deck. He was only too well aware how close to death they were and he knew more was to come. All about him in the boat men were yelling as the lights smashed and the peabulb emergency lighting cast a weak and ghastly glow upon bearded faces.

'Steer one – eight – oh,' he croaked out.

Up in the kiosk the steuermann wiped the blood from his forehead and repeated the order.

U-451 began to turn away from that deadly destroyer aloft.

During these fraught moments in which he must use all his skill and cunning to escape was no time to rage over being caught with his pants down. The bedlam around him in the livid blue light, the shriek of escaping water, the yells of a man rising to shrieks of terror and pain, the feel of the boat lurching as massive disturbances of the water continued to roil about her, all this nightmare horror had to be compartmentalised. Up there a killer was hunting him. Nightmare horrors must be thrust away back into the darkness, and Baldur Wolz must seek only the salvation of his boat and her crew.

When they were safe he would then strip the flesh off the bones of Fahnrich Ulrich Rudhart and deliver him personally to Smutje for nice fresh soup, bones, flesh, blood and all. But certainly there would be no eyes or brain, no brain or eyes at all!

U-451 turned as the rudders bit. The smells of the boat wafted, and a sudden strong whiff of cabbage caught in Wolz's nostrils. Stinks were inescapable in a boat; they were ignored or scented out. He could see the interior of the boat and the kilometres of wiring and piping, the dials and levers, the whole complicated machine, and superimposed on that he could see in his mind's eye the position of his boat in the sea, the lie of the destroyer above, the courses; see and calculate.

The destroyer had attacked from port to starboard and had dropped just that fraction too late. Now he'd turn and come in on a reciprocal. His underwater detection apparatus would be pinging away, and he'd be closed up ready for the next pattern of charges.

Wolz had instinctively turned U-451 away, heading south.

Depth?

His brain felt sluggish. Should he go up and try to trick the Yankee skipper?

Or should he dive deeper still and hope the settings on the wasserbomben would not be adjusted for greater depth?

His brain felt as though some malefic spirit was stirring in his skull with a big wooden spoon, shiny, black on the edges, greasy like those spoons they stirred the soup with in the Black Forest hotel kitchen . . .

'Take her down to one fifty, Chief.'

He spoke firmly, lifting his voice just a little. The Chief waiting for orders on the line responded with an instant,

'Very good!'

U-451 began to flood and dive deeper into the depths.

Order was regained after the immediate chaos following the first attack. This was a crew made up of the usual mix; half were old hands who had sailed with Wolz before in U-451 and the other half were new, and supposed to be battle-worthy. The truth was, Wolz had been lucky, for there were fewer raw hands than he might have expected. Admiral Dönitz had simply turned U-451 around, patched her up, and dispatched her again into American waters.

The hunting was too good and the pickings too fat to waste any time at all.

Working up had been completed on passage out, and Baldur Wolz very quickly confirmed the truth about the skipper which the old hands told the new.

'Hundred and twenty.'

Wolz nodded, his mind still figuring the angles and depths, courses and speeds.

The sound of the destroyer's screws rumbled from a dull roar to that electric shriek of a train hurtling through a station. The unnerving racket neared and passed not quite overhead. Wolz called orders that swung U-451 away from the path the pattern would take.

When they came, the wasserbomben were as unpleasant as ever. But their booming thumps through the water rolled and bellowed far enough away for the boat merely to acknowledge their effect with a small roll and a slight shudder.

Wolz did not feel as though clawed talons had released his brain; he knew the Yankee, inexperienced though he might be, would be determined. He'd come in sniffing again.

The cox'n on his rounds screwing in fresh bulbs provided a reminder of routine and discipline overcoming fear. The screaming crewman had been silenced and Wolz's very capable First Watch Officer, Fritz Gerhardt, came back to report.

'He bashed his head, skipper, that's all the physical damage.' Gerhardt, trim and compact, a complete professional U-boatman, cocked his head up. The sound of the destroyer's screws told him, as it told Wolz, that the ship up there was travelling too fast for her underwater sound apparatus to function. She'd be rushing in again hoping to drop near enough to her first pattern to catch the U-boat before she could escape.

'And, Fritz?' said Wolz, knowing there was more.

Gerhardt had said physical damage. The rest of it was not difficult to surmise.

The IWO nodded. 'Knabler, one of the new hands. He was raving, so I clipped him. Maybe he's got tin disease, maybe he's just temporarily lost his nerve.' Gerhardt's beard looked hard and trimmed. 'But he should not have been accepted for the U-boat service.'

Baldur Wolz had served and been served by incompetents. He knew that Fritz Gerhardt was effective as a U-boatman, a fine example of all that was best in German seamanship. So he just filed away the tiny idea in his head that perhaps Fritz needed a longer rest than BdU had allowed them this time.

And then, just as Wolz prepared to give the fresh orders for course, depth and speed that would avoid the next attack, Fritz Gerhardt's face twisted. He grimaced with so sudden a shock of pain his whole face changed from that of a grim and dedicated U-boatman to that of a drooling idiot.

He grabbed his guts. He let out a long shuddering sigh.

Wolz had to ignore his IWO for the time it took him to take U-451 onto a new heading, to adjust depth by thirty five metres, and to increase speed, heading south west.

Then he could turn his attention to Gerhardt.

The IWO straightened up. The blood was coming back to his face, staining above the line of beard.

'Fritz! You –'

'I'm all right, skipper. Just felt someone had kicked me in the guts.' He shook his head and blew a breath. 'Whew. That one really caught me.'

'That one?' Fritz frowned. 'You've had gut ache before, Fritz. Didn't you see the medical people?'

'Indigestion. Nothing to it. That dressed crab –'

'That was Stuckl's last tin.'

Stuckl was the new IIWO, replacing Julius Neuhaus who had gone on to commander's school. Wolz had been pleased about that, not for Neuhaus's sake but to get him out of the boat. All the same, Julius Neuhaus had been shaping up at the end.

'He swore blind he'd got it from his French tart, who had access to a private supply,' Gerhardt ran a finger around his collar under the sloppy sweater. Everyone dressed informally unless the skipper told them otherwise. 'I think he found the box on a rubbish tip.'

Wolz felt the boat around him, the feel of her through the water. The sounds of the destroyer above faded. He'd eventually be back; but by that time Wolz would be deep and on a course at his top underwater speed that should remove U-451 from immediate trouble.

Then Gerhardt, with some anger, said, 'I wouldn't put it past some French people to poison the damned tin.'

'They attempt to sabotage our boats, and fuel. Now you're suggesting Stuckl's French madam poisoned the tins of dressed crab?'

'Something twisted a dagger in my inward parts, skipper. Indigestion, yes, I have that. But this was a trifle hotter.'

'See the Sanitätsobermaat. He'll give you a powder.'

The hydrophone operator reported in then.

'Hostile Effect lost.'

'Sweep three sixty degrees, and report.'

When the full sweep had been completed no sounds were reported from the Yankee destroyer.

'That was neat, skipper.' Gerhardt congratulated Wolz on his seamanship. 'You've lost him.'

Wolz wasn't so sure.

'These Americans are green to this game, most of them. Some of them have been at it for almost a year, before they went to war with us. But they're learning fast. I think we will motor on as we are, full listening drill, and hope we clear the area before he gets down to a detailed search.'

'Well, we've seen the Yankees, rushing about the ocean at flank speed and seeing and hearing nothing –'

'That will change, Fritz.'

And now Gerhardt managed a small laugh an unfriendly observer might describe as a chuckle.

'If they have any ships left to protect by then!'

And this, of course, was the nub and reason for the whole nightmare process.

The stab of pain suffered by his IWO passed and Wolz could concentrate on his next moves.

The orders he, like the other U-boat skippers on the American coast, had been given by Admiral Dönitz were simple.

Sink tankers!

Choose big juicy targets, only sink small fry if nothing else happened along. Actively look for the fat targets, the tankers.

Admiral Dönitz, Befehlshaber der Unterseeboote, BdU, scented victory at sea in the late spring and early summer of 1942. Shipping losses suffered by the Allies had been enormous, and were increasing. The U-boat arm of the Kriegsmarine must press on, give everything they had to give, finally make the last push that would convince America that they should pull out of this war in which they had no real interest.

Once England was isolated, the puny defiance of that small island would have to cease.

Oh, yes, victory was once again very much in the air – or, rather, at sea.

Baldur Wolz knew something of the English, for he had English friends and knew a little of the Royal Navy. He would not alter the English words from in the air to at sea, for he knew what the English meant when they said something or someone was all at sea.

'Steer two-six-five,' he said. He waited for the repeat from the helmsman and then told Gerhardt, 'If they're clearing up the mess, Fritz, why don't you get your head down for a bit? Watch-keeping will resume.'

'Very good, skipper.'

What Wolz did not say, what Gerhardt did not indicate he understood, was that the IWO could take himself off to the wardroom and down a hefty slug of schnapps. That might do his guts good. It was against regulations. But at this stage of the war and his personal part in it, Baldur Wolz – perhaps with too much pride – fancied he understood enough of men and machines to know when to bend the regulations.

Reports had come in via odd channels and circuitous routes of U-boats being sunk because the on-duty personnel on the bridge were all very merry, and the watch below were all drunk and incapable. If these reports were true, they reflected badly on what was the crack service of the Kriegsmarine. Also, they portended dark days ahead for the Third Reich.

Something itched and niggled at Wolz's mind, nibbling away at the back of his brain.

Those Black Forest soup spoons, black and shiny, were hard at work puddling inside his skull.

Not overly tall, Baldur Wolz, but broad and powerfully built, with merciless eyes that could soften in friendship, and sleek blond hair immaculately combed. His square face with the sharp Germanic features wore now a look of concentration on what was irritating him.

It was simple, so simple he might have missed it even if he'd been operating at full one hundred per cent efficiency.

He'd turned almost due west.

The Yankee would guess that the U-boat he had almost caught napping on the surface would be going on station to sink the coastwise traffic.

So – he'd simply track a line due west from the place of the encounter, and meanwhile radio for support.

Wolz simply pulled the phone across and said,

'Steer two-one-oh.'

'Steer two-one-oh.'

That should take him far enough away, provided the destroyer did not return too soon.

Then he would have to consider the unpleasant business of Midshipman Ulrich Rudhart.

It would be useless for any member of the crew, least of all the skipper, to think of the task of putting U-451 back ship-shape as clearing up in the aftermath of the attack.

Until they were safely back on the surface with nothing in sight, they must never think of themselves as being in the aftermath of an attack. Attacks could continue until they were sunk. Aftermaths did not exist in the U-boat arm until the boat was sunk or safely back in base.

As for being safely on the surface . . .

'Tell Fahnrich Rudhart,' Wolz said to his IIWO, 'that I shall hold a formal inquiry.'

Rudhart was no doubt cowering away among the eels in the forward torpedo compartment.

No further reports of contact came in from the hydrophone cabinet, and Wolz began to think he had really given the American destroyer the slip. The chance of their meeting, this far out from the coast, had been so purely fortuitous as to be, quite plainly, the work of the malicious hand of fate.

With all the problems and dangers confronting a U-boat skipper, the malign hand of fate was one adversary he could well do without.

'Make revolutions for three knots. Bring us up to periscope depth, Chief. Gently.'

The Chief Engineer, an officer who kept himself to himself, said little, and did not fuss over his engines in quite the way others Wolz had known, acknowledged. The LI, the Leitender Ingenieur, might fuss or not fuss, provided he maintained the boat in top notch condition and did not irritate the skipper.

The problem of Fahnrich Rudhart remained.

U-451 had been sailing calmly on over a deserted sea, well away from her expected point of contact with her patrol zone. Wolz, subject to the discipline of the Kriegsmarine and its training philosophy, had entrusted the watch and the bridge to the midshipman. Feldwebel Rutter had been with him, a most reliable man, and just why or how the Yankee destroyer had managed to storm up and surprise the whole four-man bridge watch was a question to be resolved.

The court of inquiry would start with the Fahnrich, for although he was in that limbo of position, not a hand and not an officer, subject to warrant officer's discipline, and yet officer-potential, he would be the one to take the responsibility. That way you either made or broke the future officer.

If this was the way to run a navy, Wolz did not really care to question. All he knew was that it worked.

'Fourteen metres, skipper.'

'Thank you, Chief. Now we'll see.'

Wolz upped the periscope and checked in the habitual, mandatory, automatic and life-saving three sixty degree sweep.

Sky and surface.

Nothing in sight in the air or on the sea.

'Down periscope.'

Apart from a crewman with a headache and a bloody head, smashed crockery, a diminution in the supply of electric light bulbs, and a few uncomfortable stomachs, they'd weathered the wasserbomben attack.

Damage reports indicated nothing serious, although the confounded leak U-451 had suffered during her last trip, patched at Lorient, might not stand too many of those kind of attacks . . .

Fritz Gerhardt cocked an inquiring eye at Wolz.

Wolz shook his blond head.

'I shall need you and Stuckl, Fritz. I want to get the thing over and done with.'

The two midshipmen U-451 had shipped last voyage had been posted away to different destinations, according to their deserts. The crew had called those two Laurel and Hardy. The two new middies, Ulrich Rudhart and Josef Steidle, had not so far picked up nicknames. They would, they would, if they survived . . .

The wardroom was tidied up to a remarkable extent, loose magazines stuffed away, the gramophone covered by a cloth, no crockery whatsoever lying about. The table looked polished, bare and official.

Fahnrich Josef Steidle was posted on duty in the control

room, keeping the watch. At the slightest hint of an emergency the officers could be out of the wardroom and into the zentrale in no time at all. They'd be there quicker than a flash. Wolz sat at the table, flanked by Gerhardt and Stuckl. The cox'n wheeled Fahnrich Ulrich Rudhart in, and stood him to attention before the table. Rodl, the second wireless operator, sat at the end of the table to make the official record of the court's proceedings.

After the necessary preliminaries, Wolz said, 'This is a Court of Inquiry. I want to make perfectly sure, however, that you fully understand the powers of a Ship's Court Martial. Do you understand?'

Rudhart was a full-fleshed young man, with bloated cheeks and protruding eyes. The back of his head was not vertical; but the angle of inclination was barely apparent. He was, Wolz knew, a devoted party member, and a long time had been needed to get him to refrain from giving the Nazi salute at every opportunity. The Kriegsmarine saluted in the navy way.

'I think so –'

Wolz interrupted, and turned to Gerhardt.

'Herr Oberleutnant. Please describe briefly to the Fahnrich the powers of a Ship's Court Martial.' Wolz waited just long enough to give Gerhardt time to draw a breath, and then said, 'However, there is really only one provision, one fact, the Fahnrich need know. That is the penalty the court is empowered to inflict.'

Fritz Gerhardt had breath enough to say, 'If found guilty the accused may be executed immediately.'

'Precisely.'

Ulrich Rudhart's beefy face did not pale; but those protruding eyes protruded even more. Veins showed beside his nose.

'Now, Fahnrich, do you understand?'

'I understand, Herr Kapitänleutnant.'

'Very good. Now, before I call witnesses, have you anything to say?'

'There was a mist, Herr Kapitänleutnant.'

Wolz saw the young man intended to say more; but he cut in with, 'A mist? That can easily be verified. There were three witnesses on the bridge.'

Rudhart burst out, 'Herr Kapitänleutnant! Would you *really* shoot me?'

'Yes.'

'Order!' said the cox'n, outraged by the lad's behaviour.

What Wolz did not say, wishing to make the youngster see the gravity of what he had done – or failed to do – was that no, of course he wouldn't shoot him. Wolz was not a stupid monster in command. He wouldn't deprive himself of Rudhart's services, once the lad had been braced up. Manpower was short.

And then Wolz realised that, by God! he *was* stupid.

This kind of harassment had been employed against Wolz himself, as it had against Fritz Gerhardt, and Stuckl and just about every successful officer in the Kriegsmarine. It made a fellow brace up and think. It might put a holy breeze up his pants, and bring the sweat out on his forehead; but it made a man perform his duties better than before. At least, and here Wolz refused to ponder an old, old question, at least, that was the theory which had worked in most cases.

He'd just wanted Rudhart to understand the enormity of his crime.

For crime it was, to put your comrades and your boat in peril.

And now Wolz realised that this young man, this party member, this unfit person for the U-boat arm, had been pushed too far. And, compared with most other pushings, he'd hardly been nudged . . .

Rudhart put his hand in his pocket.

The cox'n started to voice a crisp rebuke, and then stopped.

Rudhart's hand came out of his pocket. Wolz caught a gleam of blue steel, then the Fahnrich pulled the trigger and the flat little automatic belched flame.

2

After the cox'n had flung his arms about Rudhart, holding him firmly, and Stuckl had leaped across and hit the youngster hard – very hard – they prised the automatic from his fingers.

It was a Walther PPK in 6.35-mm. The little auto, the Pistole Polizei Kriminale, was still large enough to be a menace, and in the hush after the bang and the scuffle, they all stared at the skipper.

Wolz had not moved.

He felt the responsibility. He felt some shame, and then shoved that aside as not so much being weakness as being foolish. In the tenets of the German Navy, he had nothing with which to reproach himself.

The slug had passed close to his right ear. Too damn close.

In his cold, metallic voice, Baldur Wolz said, 'He pulled to the left. I should hope that my officers would be better trained in marksmanship.'

'Skipper!' protested Gerhardt. 'If he'd shot better, you'd be – you'd be –'

'Yes, Fritz.'

And then, right in the middle of that, Gerhardt caught at his stomach and doubled up.

He spluttered out, 'I'm all right, I'm all right. Just a twinge.'

'Court adjourned, gentlemen,' said Wolz. 'Cox'n! Take the Fahnrich away and see he is safe. Stuckl! Help Fritz to his bunk. Move!'

'But I'm all right, skipper –' Gerhardt's protests were ignored by Wolz. The cox'n dragged Rudhart away, calling for hands to help carry the unconscious Fahnrich through the bulkhead doorways, and Stuckl helped Gerhardt to his bunk which was ripped out by Wolz himself. Gerhardt flopped down.

'If he'd shot you, skipper –'

'He didn't. Now lie still. Stuckl, get the Sanitätsobermaat in here. Fetch a powder.'

'Very good!'

Stuckl lumbered off. A bearish man, hard as nails, he was thinking all kinds of crazy thoughts.

Wolz guessed what Stuckl was thinking.

Hell! Hadn't Wolz dreamed and dreamed of commanding his very own boat!

He went back and picked up the gun.

Not many PPKs had been manufactured in the 6.35-mm calibre. Among the plethora of weaponry available to the SS and Gestapo, the PPK was highly regarded and popular, so Wolz understood. Somehow, he didn't altogether trust the handgun, preferring his own Walther P38. Still, here the gun was, and it had been shot full in his face, and only a trembling hand or plain incompetent shooting had caused the bullet to miss.

No doubt Rudhart's party connections had obtained the gun for him. He had most certainly smuggled it aboard, quite apart from his regulation sidearm. Wolz wondered why the Fahnrich should have done that. After all, he could scarcely have anticipated having to use it in the fashion he had ...

Wolz rubbed along with party people, recognising the valuable services they had rendered to the country. Certainly the Leader had hauled the country up out of the muck and given Germany back self-respect. All the same, he'd never joined, as had his cousins, simply because he'd been in the navy and hard at it as a serving officer. He had not regretted the way fate here had ordained what he should do.

He went through to the control room and made sure no

one had caught any funny ideas. A U-boat was a hotbed of rumour. The close confinement in which everyone lived encouraged gossip with hothouse fervour. But he could rely on the cox'n, a very steady man, to scotch the wildest stories. Come to that, the truth was wild enough.

He carried out a thorough check. He was aware of the effect the hard cold eye of the skipper had on the men. He was human enough to deplore that, and human enough to wonder just how much effect he did have. He knew he could command these men. He wondered over the effect to the extent that he really cared. He had a horror of being counter-productive.

Well, he'd certainly been all wrong with Rudhart. He could feel the intense heat burning in him, not shame – not that! But anger at himself, resentment that such a stupid thing could have happened, annoyance that the watches would now be upset.

The other Fahnrich, Josef Steidle, a fair-haired youngster with blue eyes and, spoiling that effect, a pudge of a nose, studiously kept that pudgy nose glued to his tasks. The planesmen sat squarely on and did not look up. The cox'n came back and resumed his normal duties. The Chief was right on top of his job. In all, U-451 was back in shape.

Until the next fraught incident . . .

'Up periscope!'

After the full sweep which detected nothing, and the rehousing of the *spargel*, Wolz decided that the hands could be piped to dinner.

He took U-451 down to eighty metres, and then the meal was served. There were no more tins of that dressed crab.

Gerhardt was fine, again, and he joked with Stuckl.

'Your whore gave you the works in a tin, Franz, instead of –'

'Nonsense!' burst out Stuckl. 'I'm all right – and so's the skipper –'

'I didn't eat any crab,' said Wolz, amused.

'Well, I did,' persisted the IIWO, 'And very good it was. Like Colette - mm!'

'Colette!' Gerhardt half-turned and winked at Wolz. 'Oh - I know. That's the one that wobbles when she walks, must wear something mighty loose under all that lace and frilling - you know the sort, like a badly packed freighter.'

Wolz picked up his coffee cup to hide a smile.

Stuckl bit.

'Wobble! Wobble! I tell you, Fritz, she's a firm handful, as firm as two peaches. Believe me -'

'Some people like a little movement.'

Stuckl looked bewildered. 'But you implied -'

Wolz put his coffee cup down.

'I think we must draw a median line,' he said, speaking with solemnity over so serious a subject. 'Firmness is desirable, of a surety. And so is a certain - shall we say flexibility? After all, a pair of walnuts do not do much for one, do they, now?'

'Absolutely my sentiments,' confirmed Gerhardt.

'Walnuts, wobble,' Stuckl did not sport a monocle. Which was a pity. Now, if ever, was the moment for him to screw a monocle in his eye and deliver himself of some apt rejoinder.

All he could say was, 'Colette has the welfare of the U-boatmen at heart -'

'At where?' interrupted Gerhardt with a leer.

'And I am absolutely confident the crab was harmless.'

So, after some more casual leg-pulling, the matter lapsed. Afterwards, Wolz realised again that he had proved himself stupid.

Rudhart recovered from Stuckl's blow and was locked away in the stern ends to let him cool off. Everyone realised he was for the high jump. You couldn't go around taking pot shots at the skipper.

From time to time Gerhardt would glance quickly and covertly at Wolz.

Intercepting a few of these glances, Wolz took the opportunity, in the wardroom when they were alone, to say, 'I'm all right, Fritz. The bullet missed. And I've been shot at before, you know.'

'I know, skipper. Just that –' He made a face. 'Well, just that . . .'

He trailed off.

'Don't worry about me. I've a hide like a rhinoceros.'

'I think, skipper, if he'd killed you I'd have strangled him, there and then.'

Stuckl put his head in through the bulkhead opening and caught the tail end.

He stepped through.

'Oh, no, you wouldn't, Fritz.'

'No?'

'No. I'd have bashed his head in first.'

'Yes, Franz?' said Wolz.

'Hydrophone Effect. Very faint and far off. But it's there.'

'Capital!'

Wolz went off at once to the hydrophone cabinet across the gangway from his so-called cabin behind its green curtain.

Gerhardt and Stuckl exchanged glances.

'I meant it, Franz.'

'And so did I, Fritz.'

The Hydrophone Effect was there, all right. The HE trembled on the verge of hearing. But as U-451 sailed westward, so the sound strengthened. Rodl, the second operator, was on duty, and he was a competent man.

Wolz had had to put up with incompetents in his time, and so sorted the sheep from the goats. If a man was good at his job, Wolz would make sure the man understood the skipper was aware of that.

'Sounds like a freighter, sir. Heavy and medium speed revolutions.' Rodl's sharp face creased as he listened, his head cocked inside the big headphones. 'But they could be a destroyer's screws – slow revolutions. I'll be sure in a moment.'

Wolz sweated it out. The differences in sound were minute, noticeable only by trained ears. The marvel was that so much information could be heard through the water.

Presently, Rodl looked up.

'Too thumpy for a destroyer, skipper. Freighter, for sure.'

'Good.'

Wolz slapped Rodl on the shoulder and went through to the control room.

The course correction was trifling. The freighter on oh-nine-oh would pass with an adjustment to U-451's course of ten degrees directly across the U-boat's bows. The southerly course had paid dividends . . .

The only problem was the light.

Up in the tower the helmsman acknowledged the change of course. Wolz bent to the eyepieces of the periscope.

The mandatory three sixty degree sweep had to be made first. Then Wolz could look upon his intended victim.

The light was not good.

Any idea of surfacing and sinking the ship by gunfire was banished. Anyway, he wanted to get rid of a torpedo to make more room in the fore ends. They were so crowded it was more disgusting than a brothel on Saturday night.

The ship was a large runner. She was not in convoy and was proceeding alone and unescorted.

Well, the Americans had started convoying shipping along their east coast. They'd started far too late and had paid an awful price for their pigheaded obstinacy.

But this ship was different.

She was attempting to run the U-boat blockade to England.

Wolz began to call out courses and speeds so that the attack table could work its miracle. Vectors and angles and speeds and courses, all were digested and then the answers spewed out.

'Flood tubes one and three.'

Up front in the torpedo room the hands would flood up the tubes and prepare the eels. Those beauties would pay off their costs now. Wolz would use two. Night was falling, the ship was making a good sixteen knots and if he missed with his first pattern he wouldn't get a chance of a second. He felt that.

Gerhardt called up.

'Is she a big one, skipper?'

'Ten thousand, I'd say.'

Gerhardt looked pleased. She might not be a tanker; but she was not a sprat.

U-451 could make sixteen knots on the surface, a fraction over seventeen if the Chief thrashed his diesels, and if Wolz chose to pursue the freighter to get into another firing position he'd run a long long way to the east. His task was to sink as many ships as possible, and to pick the tankers as priority targets. If he missed and then chased, he'd consume vital fuel, lose time, and generally foul up what should be a tightly-controlled operation.

He just must not miss, that was all . . .

The vessel lumbered on.

The range came down as U-451 neared the point at which the attack table indicated the torpedoes must be loosed.

Correcting all the time, keeping his wits about him, Wolz felt all his being coalescing and concentrating into this single instant in time. This was what being a U-boatman was all about. This was the moment for which everything else existed. All the training, the skills, the experience, all the money and design genius, all the planning, all the morale boosting – these now added together and delivered up this supreme moment to the U-boat commander.

And, if the eels missed, everything would have gone for nothing.

The ship's course had not deviated from the moment of first sighting. No doubt the skipper fondly imagined his superior speed of sixteen knots lent him immunity. He would shake off prowling U-boats, he would think, and disdain their torpedoes. Wolz stared through the periscope and called out the angles and bearings, the range, and his mind checked and double-checked.

Over to starboard the sea was stained orange by the setting sun. The water ahead looked dark, glittering with streaks of random fire. The night breathed warm up there, filled with the beauty of the sinking sun. It would be a fine day tomorrow.

And Baldur Wolz lined up his sights on a splendid ship and prepared to send her to the bottom.

He had long since got over his repugnance. Yet he never would really overcome his feelings of horror at sinking great vessels and in the process possibly killing other men. It was the job for which he had been trained, but that did not excuse it. It was quite simply all he personally could do to bring this war to a speedy conclusion.

The quicker the Allies were brought to their senses, the quicker the war would be over. And the best way of making them see sense was to cut the life lines, and that meant sinking ships.

The last few necessary corrections were fed in. U-451 moved through the water, a long, lean, deadly steel shark.

Baldur Wolz took a breath.

The sights came on.

'Tube one.' He waited. Then, '*Loose!*'

A moment only to allow for a small angular spread, and then, 'Tube three. *Loose!*'

The two thumps as the torpedoes sprang from the launching tubes, the slight lurch of the boat, the hiss of compressed air as the Chief flooded to compensate . . . Wolz glued his eyes to the scope.

Then, mindful of his duty, he took a sweep all around the compass. Just in case.

But no dark dot broke the hostile horizon line.

As was always the case, the men with the stop watches held them as though clutching race track betting slips. Everyone else counted.

Those in the boat who could not see what was going on above – and that was everyone except the skipper – held themselves tautly, in a suspense of waiting.

And then they heard the skipper simply say, 'Prepare to surface.'

And they waited.

Watching his target across that sunset sea, Wolz saw, a moment after he had loosed his eels, what the ship up there did.

She turned.

She could not be aware of the doom that sped towards her just beneath the surface.

But she turned.

She swung ten degrees to port, heading in towards the U-boat.

The torpedoes would now bubble harmlessly past.

That last second turn, after he had loosed, had completely spoiled the aim.

Baldur Wolz had missed.

How he kept calm, his voice equable, unruffled, he did not know. He felt like – like –

'Prepare for gun action. Close up gun's crew.'

Instantly a scramble began as the gun's crew mustered and the flooring was ripped up to break open the 8.8-cm ammunition magazine. The men looked pained.

The skipper had missed!

Now they had to shoot the damned enemy vessel out of the water with their marksmanship.

Wolz offered no explanation.

No one was foolhardy enough to ask him for one.

Certainly, Fritz Gerhardt knew his skipper well enough by now to know something odd had happened. Baldur Wolz just did not miss sitting targets.

Gerhardt came to the obvious, and correct, conclusion.

He spoke quietly to Stuckl.

'The cheeky fellow zig-zagged. That has to be it. After we loosed.'

'Yes,' said Stuckl.

The long brass cylinders of the cartridge cases passed up hand to hand, the shells polished and efficient, sleek with power packed into a deadly punch. The fixed ammunition for the 8.8-cm was not light; but the way the gun ammunition numbers handled it they made the job seem as though they were tossing French loaves to one another.

There was no argument over who was going to handle the deck gun. Fritz Gerhardt had taken a personal pleasure in stroking their new gun, for the old one had succumbed to an unpleasant underwater hazard to be found in wartime. The new weapon was going to be shot by the IWO, and no one was going to argue the point with him.

Wolz was perfectly satisfied with that arrangement.

Unless, as he might, he took the decision to captain the gun himself.

The Chief brought the boat up smoothly. Swirls of white water rolled away from her casing and deck, washing redly on her starboard side, dark and cavernous on her port. U-451 broke through the surface and settled down. Baldur Wolz was the first man up the ladder and out onto the bridge.

3

The night breathed about them warm and strong with the scent of the sea.

The diesels rumbled through the fabric of U-451 and her sharp prow cut a swathe of tumbled white water.

Over there, turning away from the track of the two eels, the freighter lumbered on. She looked gaunt and unlovely with her stern and side reflecting the last of the sunset, lurid orange and vermilion patches highlighting the shrouding shadows.

No lights showed. Well, at least, Wolz reflected, they'd learned something else besides convoys since he was last in these waters.

The gun crew sprang out onto the fore casing and cast the gun loose. They were ready for action in a time that marginally pleased Wolz. They'd do better, given time and even more intensive training.

He watched carefully as Fritz Gerhardt removed the tompion . . .

The target bore on. She was a sizeable ten thousand tonner, all right; but as a target she would need skill to ensure hits enough to sink her. Wolz gave a small course correction after he had transferred control to the bridge and the boat eased away a few points to give the gun better clearance. The first shell slid into the breech.

The smell of the sea was almost overpoweringly strong after the stink inside the boat. The smell of diesel and the taint of exhaust fumes were banished.

Wolz said in a quiet, normal voice, 'Open fire as soon as you are ready.'

'Very good!'

U-451 surged on, going up and down, riding the swell with a spreading wash of white suds from her saddle tanks.

Aft on the wintergarden the flak crew were closed up and ready to cut loose with their 2-cm. By his course correction, Wolz had opened up their field of fire. They would be useful, those little 2-cm shells, in smashing up the freighter's wireless cabin, and preventing her from sending out a sub-sighting.

Although, and here Wolz harked back to the early days of the war, although these days and out here in the Atlantic, he'd be long gone before anyone came around in answer to the distress call.

The 8.8 opened up. The first shot, hard and flat, cracked out.

The lance of flame, vivid in the dusk, pointed directly at the target. The concussion boomed and bellowed.

Wolz looked across.

That would wake them up!

Where the shot went he had no idea.

The gun crew slammed the breech open, the next round slammed in, the breech closed, the men waited as the layer took careful aim, and then – *blam!*

Quite clearly, on the black hull of the ship, a rose of flame jetted before instantly disappearing. Smoke lifted.

A hit.

Wolz refrained from comment. Fritz Gerhardt knew what he was about. He knew where to hit a ship to sink her.

The next three shots all blammed out with lurid tongues of flame and smashing concussions, and then the ship began to turn.

She turned away, showing her stern, turning to starboard so as to get away from her tormentor. And, also, as Wolz knew, so as to bring her stern deck gun into action.

He had no real fear that his earlier experience with a random shot from a deck gun would be repeated. U-451 was so small a target, low and slender against the dark sea, her conning tower a hump of darkness amid darkness, that the gunners on the fantail of the ship would hardly see him at all. Their only real aiming mark would be the flashing discharge of his own gun.

Gunsmoke wafted past his head, and the acrid bite in his nostrils and throat did not overly displease him.

U-451 rolled with the swell and as she righted so the 8.8 barked again. If Gerhardt didn't sink or disable her very soon now, Wolz would have to think of turning on a pursuit course. With this in mind he bent to the pipe and gave orders to the flak gun's crew.

'Open fire. Hose him down to start with – if he shoots back, concentrate on the gun.'

'Very good!'

The sharp metallic cracks of the 2-cm broke into the more sonorous bellowings of the 8.8, although that gun was, as everyone knew, a low-trajectory, hard-hitting spiteful terror of a weapon.

Sparkles broke along the upperworks of the freighter. She was turning now so that she was three quarters on and still they hadn't loosed off with their deck gun over there. Black smoke, massive and heavy against the distant sky, rose from her funnel, and the ruby light caught and polished in brilliance the turning flank of the ship.

The picture was very pretty. Wolz just wanted to sink the ship and then resume night sailing stations.

Gerhardt urged his crew on, and the 8.8 slammed again.

The lance of flame from the gun muzzle, the splash of smoke, had just registered on Wolz's retinas when he was blinded by the light.

He shut his eyes.

Light, searing heat, and almost immediately after an enormous bang. And then a rushing wind, ripping and tearing at him.

U-451 rolled like a goaded horse.

Men yelled, unheard in the roar, and clung for support.

Wolz opened his streaming eyes.

The ship was gone.

'Poor devils!'

The detonation continued to ring and clash in his ears. His head vibrated. He could hear nothing.

Bits and pieces began to fall from the sky after a time, splashing soundlessly into the sea.

A chunk of iron plate hit the deck and caromed in silent slow-motion off the casing and spun off into the sea.

Wolz shook his head.

That ship had been no ordinary freighter.

An ammunition ship.

She'd been hit in a vital spot and – *whammy!* – up she'd gone.

After a time, when hearing returned and men could talk to one another again, the awful finality of that infernal explosion weighed on the mind. The speed with which so many men had been killed – gone to their Creator in the jargon of another time – impressed and depressed the hands.

Everyone was in subdued mood as U-451 sailed on. Wolz took her into the area of the explosion.

Some wreckage was located, spars, a few fragments of a lifeboat that could never have had a chance to be used, a lifebelt.

The lifebelt was hooked in and hauled up dripping onto the casing.

'SS *Andalfo*, skipper,' called up Gerhardt.

A knife scraped away white paint to reveal the name.

Wolz nodded and called down to Fahnrich Steidle to fetch the book.

The silhouette and the name revealed beside other details of their victim the all-important fact that she had been of 9,450 GRT.

Wolz nodded sombrely.

No one was going to get over the impression created by the destruction of SS *Andalfo* in a hurry.

Except the skipper.

Baldur Wolz braced himself up.

This kind of atrocity was what he was at sea to make

happen. He did not like it. He could be honest with himself now. He'd done enough, proved enough, so that no one could accuse him of slackness. But he didn't have to like what he was forced to do to bring the war to a close.

The voice Baldur Wolz used to give the orders to resume watches and turn onto the two-seven-oh heading and proceed at twelve knots on the surface – all simple decisions dictated by time and position – that voice sounded, to use a descriptive phrase much in vogue at the time, like a graveyard gate on a rusty hinge ...

With his crew now in better spirits, with two eels gone from the forward messdeck and that bit of extra room afforded by the reloads appearing enormous, with a goodly sinking already, and with the prospect of an undisturbed night ahead, Wolz could make an attempt to sleep.

But, of course, he could not.

For some reason he began to think back on all the comrades he had known, good friends in the service, bastard enemies in the service. He thought of his English friends in the Royal Navy and of the tragic death of one of them. He thought of girls.

For Baldur Wolz thoughts of deeds with, and love of, girls were naturally occurring phenomena. He could not envisage a life without ladies. Mind you, there were some very nasty and vicious people calling themselves women, and he'd met one or two, to his own misfortune. But in the main, Baldur Wolz and girls got along fine.

Like Irmgard.

Irmgard had a walk that just by existing focussed a fellow's eyeballs. He'd stare at that undulating rear until Irmgard passed out of his line of vision. Talk of rabbits and snakes was quite insufficient. So said the stories of Irmgard.

Wolz sat up on his bunk and reached for the water carafe. His mouth was dry. The water was not too bad, grade A for drinking, and the condenser was operating efficiently. It was not like a fine Rhenish wine, however ...

Taking scant heed of rules and regulations, Wolz had on

this trip brought a magnum of his Uncle Siegfried's best French champagne aboard. The magnum, cased securely, reposed now under his bunk. It was reserved for a special occasion Wolz trusted would not long be delayed.

He lay back again, thinking of champagne and of Irmgard, who was Gretchen's friend. Gretchen, who was tall and willowy and sometimes despaired of what she called her skinniness, could wear black lace in such a way as to inflame a man to instant action. Wolz had pulled Gretchen out of a hole in the ice. The hole had been black and freezing and quite simply a place of horror for a U-boatman to dive into.

He and Gretchen had seen what they could do together during the winter evenings and nights to make up for that moment of horror. Wolz smiled reflectively.

The sheepskin rug before the log fire proved to be a favourite place for Gretchen to display the raw arrogant power of her body in the black lace and black stockings. The enormous bed with its eiderdowns, also, proved capital. They'd spent a fine old time romping. Quite. Wolz had thought of Lottie and Heidi and the others at the time, of course; but they were not here in this Black Forest hotel, and Gretchen was.

And then Irmgard, who was Gretchen's dear friend, came to stay.

Well, now . . .

The reflective smile on Wolz's face as he lay on his bunk in U-451 was not quite a leer. Not quite. The difference separating that pleased smile from a leer was of the order of difference separating a submarine from a U-boat.

He had thought of Mimi and Lottie and Heidi and the others, including his uncle's secretary, Mariza Kalman, and then allowed himself to delight in Gretchen. He had forced away all thoughts of Trudi von Hartstein. For her, his feelings were jumbled, miserable, forlorn, lecherous and respectful. He had got over the terrible experience of seeing her face, all gaunt and desperate, as he made love to other women. Trudi was a true mystery. But he could romp with Gretchen on the sheepskin rug and actually see Gretchen's face instead of the ghostly image of Trudi . . .

With the dawn U-451 ran into a mild breeze. The sea stretched in immensity about them, streaked in ruffling strokes of blue and green, with hardly a dot of white anywhere. The sky drifted with a few high patches of cloud. The air in its sea freshness managed to overcome the ever-present stink of the diesels. This was a day for living.

Also, as ever, if an enemy ship hove in sight, it would be a fine day for dying.

Wolz's white cap cover gleamed brilliantly in the early sunlight.

He stood on his bridge, perched above the run of the sea over the saddle tanks, feeling the motion of his command through the water, and he felt as good and bright as a man had any right to feel in the midst of an unholy war.

The figures of the watch on the bridge held rigidly to their stations. They were positioned according to a plan. A U-boat running on diesels was unable to use her massive array of listening devices, so that the first contact would be visual. And, even here, still not yet within striking distance of the American coast, eyes must continually look aloft for the patrolling aircraft . . .

The Chief reported his fuel figures.

For a Type VII boat to operate at all so far from her base at Lorient all manner of ingenious tricks had to be employed to extend the range. The fore ends were just simply packed with gear and supplies. Some of the water tanks were filled with fuel. If the condenser broke down, as could happen, the men would be in for a tough time. Also, on this trip Wolz had had the reassurance of a promise of a refuelling operation. If this did turn out as promised, and there seemed no reason to suppose otherwise, the milch cow would give U-451 a fresh radius of action.

The idea pleased Wolz from an operational point of view.

But from the point of view of getting back home and finding out what had happened to Trudi the idea was not so rosy . . .

Trudi von Hartstein – why was she so infuriating?

Well, he was about to go below and see about coffee when the lookout hailed.

Wolz trained his glasses on the distant spot on the western horizon.

Smoke.

A ship, sailing grandly up towards them over the curve of the world, sailing on into the jaws of death.

Somehow, as he gave orders to prepare for action, Wolz took little comfort from the encounter.

4

Two factors impelled Wolz towards his next course of action.

No. If he was honest with himself, three factors were involved.

One was that promise of a refuelling and re-arming operation.

The second was the desire on his part to give Fritz Gerhardt more practical experience. Gerhardt had been through a commander's course, and his periscope school had fitted him for command. Wolz would lose his IWO on the next trip, for Gerhardt would have his own boat.

Wolz wanted Gerhardt to succeed. He might not be in quite the same class as Kern Ehrenberger; but he was a fine man and officer.

The third reason Wolz did not care to contemplate. It was obvious enough to him, even if Dönitz might have failed to understand.

When he told him, Gerhardt's face expressed only surprised pleasure. But, looking at his IWO, Wolz saw more than that. Gerhardt was ecstatic. This was a shrewd move on the part of the skipper of U-451.

Fritz Gerhardt took the bridge. The skipper went below to handle the attack table.

The myriad controls and dials, levers and tubing suddenly came at Wolz in an entirely fresh light. Yet, not so much fresh light as a resurrection of the time before he had achieved command, when he had been a IIWO and a IWO, and had lived in the bowels of the boat during an attack.

He shook his head. Well, this time it was all up to Gerhardt. Wolz knew that the First Watch Officer would not let him down.

The attack progressed smoothly, according to the procedures laid down. The boat manoeuvred herself into the best position to narrow the angle. The range steadily came down. The tubes up forward were flooded, numbers two and four this time.

Gerhardt gave his orders and readings in a firm voice.

Of course Wolz was concerned over this action. It could so easily be construed in the wrong light. Also, and much more importantly, despite all his fine fellow feelings for Fritz Gerhardt, Wolz was still in his own eyes hazarding his boat.

That went so much against the grain he had to make a deliberate effort to refrain from saying: 'All right, Fritz. Well done. I'll take over now.'

That had not been his intention, and Gerhardt knew it.

Willy nilly, he had to ride with the outcome of this attack.

But, naturally, it would be successful! Of course it would!

But it wasn't.

At the crucial moment Fritz Gerhardt doubled up with an agonised yell. His face contorted. He gripped his stomach in twisting fists. He turned leprous grey. And blood ran from between his lips.

The eels went anywhere or nowhere.

Certainly, they did not sink the freighter.

Almost unconscious, trying not to writhe in pain, Gerhardt was brought down into the wardroom. Wolz had to ignore his IWO except to yell, 'Get the Sanitätsobermaat!'

Then he was at the eyepiece of the scope.

The freighter looked enormous, almost on them, a white bone between her teeth somehow ludicrously impossible in such a large lumbering steamer.

'Prepare to surface!' bellowed Wolz. 'Gun action! *Move*!'

The freighter was passing on her course and soon she'd be quarter on. U-451 would have to look sprightly to catch her.

Spurred on by the events of the past few moments and well knowing what failure would incur, the hands broke out the ammunition and cast loose the 8.8 the moment U-451 surfaced. Wolz scrambled up onto the bridge, transferred command, and glared at the target.

She was turning away, with a head start, and he could plainly see the tiny figures running aft. Her gun crew would shoot all right. They might merely be a nuisance; but they were an added hazard Wolz had to figure into the equation.

In these few moments he had time to call down the pipe.

'Fritz? How is he?'

Stuckl's voice echoed up.

'Not good, skipper. The Sanitätsobermaat has no real idea what it is – perforated ulcer, appendicitis – but he does say that Fritz needs a doctor.'

'Indigestion!' swore Wolz.

U-451 picked up speed as the diesels worked up the revolutions. She began to tremble and hurl herself through the sea, a steel shark on the heels of her prey.

'Where do we find a doctor here?' growled Wolz.

And then the obvious answer occurred to him. He eyed the freighter. She was a fine big ship, a fast vessel even to have her skipper contemplate running without convoy. She'd have a doctor aboard.

He bent to the pipe.

'Chief. I need every revolution you have. Every last one.'

'Well now, Skipper –'

The Chief knew his engines. He'd nursed U-451 back home after her last patrol. He knew what they would do. They'd had to perform some very fast manoeuvring last trip and the engines, although overhauled, were not in the shape they should be in. Wolz knew that. The Chief, bearing in mind his responsibilities, would not let the skipper forget.

'We have to catch a ship. Have to. She'll have a doctor aboard. Fritz needs a doctor and his facilities.' Wolz swallowed. 'I'll let you know if she outruns us. If necessary, couple in the motors.'

The Chief's voice came back hard and decisive.

'Very good!'

U-451 pounded on over the sea, an ambulance chasing a hospital.

Twelve passengers was the maximum number allowed to be carried before you ran into problems of regulations demanding the provision of extra accomodation and extra life-saving equipment. So passenger cargo liners more often than not contained cabins for twelve passengers.

T. R. Antrobus, master of MV *Cotash*, whilst usually welcoming the diversion afforded by different types of people in his ship and taking their meals at his table, sometimes wished them to Halifax and gone. As now.

This bunch, being sailed back to England, really got up his nose. His nose was large, florid, bounteous, and a terror at sniffing out misdeeds among the miscellany of rogues and rascals comprising his crew. The nose belonging to T. R. Antrobus was like its possessor, and his ample form filled his blue uniform and strained the brass buttons. He liked salt water, did Tom Antrobus, and he didn't much care for milk-sops, and folk who used perfume.

And just as he'd gained command of *Cotash*, a splendid vessel, they'd started this damned stupid war.

Cotash herself was a passenger liner launched in 1937 and completed the following year, and she was a honey. She had twin screws powered by sixteen thousand h.p. giving her a speed of a fraction under seventeen knots. She was a real high-stepper. Of fourteen thousand tons gross, she possessed a clear run of stowage capacity, for all the accommodation in shelter decks did not interfere with that most important aspect of her function. The passengers were mere garniture, added to afford some slight additional advantages. As far as Antrobus was concerned, they lived like lords and didn't appreciate that fact.

He smoked a black bulldog with what his friends said was kerbside twist, and no one stood to leeward of T.R. Antrobus when his pipe was alight.

Now he glared back from the bridge wing across the neatly arranged deck, past the funnel, over the fantail with that blasted six inch popgun, at the thin evil shape of a damned Jerry U-boat.

The thing had popped up and was quite clearly intent on sinking him.

Antrobus saw the gun crew clustering, saw that pallid female, Miss Prothero, scurrying along with her parasol up as though that would stop a damned kipper, and he crunched down on the stem of his pipe and went back into the centre bridge.

He fairly bellowed down the voice pipe.

'Chief! There's an unholy U-boat chasing us. If you want to see the Gorbals or wherever it is again, then turn your damned engines over faster than they've ever gone before.'

The broad accent floated up.

'It's Interluchty, as you damned-well know, you ignorant pudge of a Sassenach. And I'll blow the engines to Halifax and gone before I'll have you say a word against them.'

They got on, did T. R. Antrobus and his Chief Engineer, Angus Macbright. They got on.

When they didn't get on each other's whatsits.

The U-boat kept on coming, and so far she hadn't taken a shot at them that Antrobus had seen. He bent a glowering frown on the bridge duty watch. They stayed glued to their tasks. *Cotash* was a modern ship, and Antrobus had expected to sail her for many years, until either they made him Commodore of the line or he retired to Southsea and the boarding house run by his widowed sister. Antrobus had never married, not caring for the perfumery side of females.

And now this stupid war had started. And they'd said you have a fine fast ship, Captain Antrobus. You can outrun any submarines. Ha!

He was carrying machine tools and bits and pieces of this and that, and there'd be nylons and cigarettes and spam and God knew what stuffed away in a hundred hidey holes. He wouldn't put it past those three young rips of cadets to have bananas secreted away. *Cotash* was fast enough.

As for the khaki-uniformed army men aboard, Antrobus just didn't want to know. The DEMS gunners were bad enough.

They fussed over a three incher with which he doubted they could hit a barrage balloon. Even if they stuck the gun muzzle up against the rubberised flank.

God damn army!

And what a collection he had aboard. There was that stuck-up major, who wore mufti all the time, and couldn't pronounce an R to save his life. There were the two American airmen who were going over to join the Eighth Air Force and who were barred from flying for health reasons. I ask you, Antrobus asked himself. Airmen who couldn't fly! And as for the snooty young Lieutenant Commander, RN. He looked at everything appertaining to the Merchant Navy as though he should wear rubber gloves and touch with a ten foot pole. Then Antrobus softened, and yielded. Well – that Mary Parson was all right, well, he amended, probably all right, for a girl.

He sighed.

U-boats and guns and torpedoes had little to do with the brilliance of Mary Parson's eyes or the trimness of her figure, or the silvery delight of her laugh.

Damn little.

Cotash was now creaming along at sixteen knots.

Antrobus called down the pipe.

'Chief! Who's got hold of yours? What's holding you back?'

The Scottish voice sounded less offensive.

'I dinna ken, laddie. I'm working on it. Leave me be for a while, and I'll let ye know.'

Slamming the whistle back, Antrobus looked savage.

More from the tone of voice than the impertinent insubordinate words, he guessed something was wrong in the stokehold. No, the engine room. They didn't have stokeholds now they used oil. He rubbed his chin. Right now, it had to happen. Right now the engines or some other God-forsaken piece of equipment in the stokehold had to go wrong – just when they were being chased by an evil stinking damned U-boat.

He looked at cadet Wheelwright and the youngster blushed like a girl having her bottom pinched.

'Cadet! Get along aft and kindly ask that Sergeant why he hasn't sunk that damned U-boat!'

'Aye aye, sir,' stuttered Wheelwright, all pink ears and drippy nose, and white patches, and he scuttled off like a spider.

The aft six inch gun chose that moment to shoot.

It left fly with a thunderous great bellow and a wash of smoke. Antrobus jumped. Damned cannons!

But he walked off to the bridge wing very smartly to see the effect of the shot.

And he did see. A short-lived plume of white spouting from the sea miles away. At least, nowhere near the U-boat.

'Can't they shoot straight?' he demanded of no one in particular. 'What do they teach 'em in the army these days? Apart from running away.'

But he knew that wasn't really fair.

He should have had his own crew members on the gun. He always had done so. Still, *Cotash* was regarded as a ship worthy of having a six incher manned by a mixed bag of marines, soldiers and sailors. The soldiers on the DEMS three incher could not depress their weapon sufficiently to hit anything lower than a diving Stuka.

They'd wanted to put a contraption aboard that worked by steam and a thing that shot a trailing bundle of wire. He'd chucked the monstrosity over the side a few days out and reported it lost in a gale.

The gun barked again.

'He's not shooting back, sir,' ventured the First Mate. James Ogilvie was a most correct man, rather on the tall and thin side, who mourned the fact that he was not allowed to grow a moustache and did not fancy the full set. But he knew his job. Of course, had he not done so, Antrobus would have rejected him with flowery language.

'He can't kipper us, can he, mister? Not from there. And maybe his gun won't work properly, going like that.' Antrobus rubbed his chin. 'All the same, you'd think he would try a crack at us.'

The six incher smacked off another one.

The First Mate said, 'I'll wager a month's pay we never hit him.'

He had no takers.

The hands said that if a steward dropped a plate in the pantry, the old man could feel it through the soles of his feet.

Now Tom Antrobus felt the checking in their progress through the soles of his feet. He checked the speed at once.

The automatic log told him *Cotash* was making fifteen knots through the water.

He roared at the pipe.

'You misbegotton leavings of a Gorbals . . . Chief! We're losing way. What in hell are you playing at?'

Macbright sounded aggrieved and aggressive.

'Inverluchty, man, Inverluchty! And the fuel pump needs to be stripped down –'

'We can't stop engines now!'

'You'll nae get any more speed from yon port shaft. It's all the fault o' –'

'Spare me your excuses. What can you *do*?'

A slight pause followed. Then,

'Pray?'

The lookout at that moment chose to call out, 'The submarine is gaining on us. She's –'

Antrobus slammed the whistle back. He shoved his brass-bound peak cap back on his head. He had a cropped thatch of greying hair, and his forehead looked like a port riding light.

He stormed out onto the bridge wing. The damned U-boat had gained on them. Now she was quite clearly going faster through the water.

Antrobus did not wish to be kippered. He did not wish to get the hammer. Up in the wireless shack the Marconi operator was sending out the regulation SOS call. But Sparks would know, as everyone else knew, no help was going to reach *Cotash* before she sank.

And still the Jerry had not shot at them ...

He turned and stomped up to peer through the screen forward. If there was a fog, a mist even ... The sea and sky smiled away, with a few dimpled clouds, and the sun shone ...

Oh, damn, damn, damn!

The absence of a certain sound brought him raging back.

'Why has the gun stopped shooting?'

No one seemed to know and then, like a devil from a stage trapdoor, cadet Wheelwright re-appeared. His face bore the remnants of a blush put there since the strain implanted by the master's orders.

'Sir!'

'Spit it out, laddie, spit it out.'

'Yessir!'

'Constipated, at your age! *Well?*'

'Sir – the U-boat is out of range –'

'Out of range!'

'I mean, they can't traverse the gun to bear, sir.'

A moment's thought convinced Tom Antrobus of the truth of this statement. He looked over the side again.

The U-boat now ran on, paralleling their course, and edging in.

'What's the devil playing at now?'

The First Mate, very arch, said, 'Shall I issue sidearms, sir? He may try to board –'

Antrobus stared at his First Officer as though the fellow was bereft of his senses.

'This, mister, is the Second World War. We are not at Trafalgar.'

'No, sir, of course not, sir. But –'

First Officer James Ogilvie pointed.

Antrobus lumbered about like a bull to look.

The U-boat was now quite deliberately taking a course that would bring her right into *Cotash.* The six inch gun on the fantail and the three inch ack-ack could not reach.

T. R. Antrobus seriously began to consider if he should fetch the key to the armoury . . .

Over the noise of the ship the voice reached them.

They went out onto the bridge wing to hear better.

'Whoever the bastard is, he speaks good English,' said Antrobus sourly.

'Ahoy there! English ship, ahoy!'

Cadet Wheelwright was at Antobus's side and he brought a loudhailer. Astonished, Antrobus took it. He raised it to his lips.

'What d'you want, you murdering bastard?'

'A little politeness? Stop the ship.'

'Stop –'

'You know the law of the sea, captain. Stop your ship or I will blow you out of the water!'

5

Keeping the passengers out of the way just did not seem worth the effort to T. R. Antrobus as the sick man was brought aboard.

The passengers clustered against the rails, looking on as the seamen went to work.

You had to hand it to these Jerry sailors, even if they were barbarous Nazi butchers. They were damned fine seamen. They got the line across and the stretcher all strapped up came whisking across the carefully gauged gap of sea in real nautical style. Anyway, the Jerry was sick and so he was out of it for a bit, and the law of the sea demanded, apart from stopping when threatened that your civilian passengers might be drowned, that you care for the sick and wounded.

In the event the Jerry skipper and Antrobus did not have *Cotash* stopped dead in the water. They maintained a steady and careful five knots so as to give the vessels control. Water splashed and ran between the hulls, one tall and studded with scuttles, lofting immense, and the other low and lean and awash with suds.

Even at five knots, on the low side, the operation was not overly difficult. Just that Antrobus had difficulty in equating monsters who sank innocent ships without warning with smart sailorly men.

The man they hauled aboard looked ghastly.

The doctor, a pale-faced prawn with spectacles, recently qualified, took one look and went to his kind of work. His name was Doctor Raisin, and he gave Antrobus the pip, not a difficult task. But he seemed to know what he was doing.

Then the man wearing the white cap on the U-boat's conning tower hailed again.

'I am sending a party aboard, captain. Remember to treat them correctly.'

'I know,' bellowed Antrobus back across the gap. 'Or I'll be shot.'

'Yes.'

The baldness of that answer shook even salt-water T.R. Antrobus.

Baldur Wolz turned away from shouting across at the English ship to give the order that would send Stuckl and a party of armed men to keep an eye on Fritz Gerhardt.

That short monosyllable conveyed exactly what the skipper of U-451 meant. This was, for the moment at least, no longer an act of war. Until the English doctor over there patched up Gerhardt and the IWO could be returned to U-451, as far as Wolz was concerned the war was in abeyance.

He just did not consider what BdU would say. He'd send back his regular wireless report as and when, and think about that problem then.

After all, if a U-boat commander could send a clear wireless message addressed to Winston Churchill saying that a ship was sinking, anything was possible in the war at sea . . .

The Chief came on the line.

'Yes, Chief?'

'Can you come down to the diesel engine room, skipper?'

Whilst it would be an exaggeration to say that an icy hand gripped Wolz's heart, the feeling he experienced was very similar. He had one of his long, black and foul cheroots in his mouth. These were obtained from Uncle Siegfried. Wolz habitually had one in the corner of his mouth, arrogantly uptilted. Alight or merely being chewed on, that jutting cigar added to the picture his men formed of him.

Now he bit through the cigar, took it away and hurled it overboard.

'Very good. I'm on my way.' He turned and saw Fahnrich Josef Steidle.

'Take the bridge. Report any signals from the party in the

English ship at once. At once. Understood?'

'Understood, skipper.'

With that, Wolz took himself down the ladder and off to see what mischief the Chief had uncovered in the diesel engine room.

If Steidle was to become a halfways decent officer he would have to stand a full watch now that Gerhardt was *hors de combat*.

The icy hand clutching his heart clutched tighter as the Chief spoke. The crouching men, the stink of diesel fuel, the feel of the closeness of the boat with the diesels bulking, one each side of the central gangway, the angular juttings of levers and pipes, the gleam of oiled machinery; all of it appeared to Wolz to rise up and smother him.

'That last high speed dash has done it, skipper. Look!'

Wolz looked. He knew enough to know that the port diesel was in bad shape.

'I'll work on it and I'll take a whip to the machinists. But it's going to be a long job. And,' added the Chief, 'this time I don't think it is iron filings.'

'But you do suspect sabotage?'

'It is possible. I'll know more when we've taken her down.'

'Carry on, then, Chief.'

'Very good!'

The raw stink of the boat got up Wolz's nostrils as he went back to the control room. After that breath of fresh air aloft he felt the aroma in the boat strongly. Did they all stink like this?

The gun crews were no doubt enjoying the fresh air.

Wolz decided to get the men up a few at a time to take advantage of this unlikely and improbable respite. He had no fear of being caught by aerial patrols – or, rather, little fear. Any surface patrol should be detected in time for him to submerge and make enough distance to put him outside detection range. In theory. But whilst he had to remain with

Cotash for Gerhardt's sake, he might as well make the most of it.

This whole business of sickness and disease struck Wolz in a new and odd light. You had a skeleton, a frame of bones, angular and gaunt, and you just strung it together with muscles and sinews to power it along, and hung a heart and lungs inside to provide the fuel and distribute the energy. And you had to add a stomach to digest up whatever your power source was, and then, having done all that, you had a perambulating framework of bones. The tricky bit was putting a brain into the skull riding at the top of the heap. You had to have that to give some kind of control. Trouble was, brains started to get other ideas, and then all kinds of trouble followed.

These morbid thoughts amused Wolz.

Having done all that, you were then stupid enough to allow some microscopic bug to come along and ruin all your handiwork. A pretty poor sort of creator, you'd think, to make a fine piece of work and then let it go to rot ...

Fritz would be all right. He had to be. That pasty-faced doctor Wolz had watched through his glasses would know what to do, and do it, and Gerhardt would return to U-451 full of smiles.

Cotash rode smoothly, affording a lee to U-451, and the lines linking the two vessels sagged and tautened with a metronomic rhythm. The breeze remained kind. Nothing untoward came in from the German party aboard the English ship.

The intriguing thought occurred to Baldur Wolz that he might take a little jaunt. He might, himself, go across to the English vessel. After all, he would not be out of his command for more than an hour ...

Intriguing.

Very ...

These hours spent idling were a fallow period. They did not please him. His task to sink enemy vessels was not being prosecuted with the fervour demanded by Dönitz.

He gave orders for provisions to be brought off *Cotash*. This was piracy, stealing, theft – call it what you will. To Wolz it was the spoils of war. Anyway, he'd have to sink *Cotash* when Gerhardt was all right ...

Funny – he hadn't really thought that before, hadn't faced the prospect.

But he would have to.

He would.

It was his duty.

Deliberately, he turned his thoughts away from a duty that called on him to sink a fine vessel and cast her crew and passengers adrift in the open ocean.

Acting according to the strict principles of submarine warfare that had now been abrogated, Stuckl had obtained a copy of the Bills of Lading and sent the details back to the U-boat. Most of it was useful war fodder. Most of the cargo would be employed to kill Germans. Machine tools to manufacture more weapons of war and the machines that made weapons were far too valuable to be allowed to enter an English port.

If Baldur Wolz did not sink this fine ship, then her cargo would be used to kill Germans.

At least, he would have the consolation of being able to see her entire complement and passengers safely into their lifeboats before he sent her to the bottom.

He put a hand through his smooth blond hair. He was tired. Tired of fighting and killing. He wondered when it had all begun, this warring between men, and fancied it must have started when men acquired possessions. Before that, in a hunter-gatherer culture, everything was held in common, so there was little need to quarrel. That was why the perambulating skeleton with the heart and lungs and the controlling brain had managed to survive. Co-operation was the key to the success of Homo sapiens. Now the damn fool was busy blowing himself up.

The watches changed.

The sun shone, the breeze blew, and Baldur Wolz took himself off to his green-curtained cubby in the corner of the wardroom to sprawl on his bunk and brood. The latest news said that Gerhardt had taken the operation well, that he was still unconscious, and that the doctor gave him a very good chance of complete recovery. Wolz nodded and went back to his bunk, and his troubled thoughts of Trudi von Hartstein.

Mystery girl, taunting him with things she knew and would not confide in him - and yet, not really taunting. She had responded to him, and used him unashamedly when she had to. He'd driven a car down to Switzerland for her. He still did not know what that had been all about. He did not think she was in the business of assisting escaping Jews. That she would be perfectly capable of doing that he did not doubt. Jewish people kept on disappearing. One day they'd be there, in their shop or house, and the next gone. They were running away from the hatred for them inspired by the party, that was true, and preferring to escape rather than go to a work camp where the authorities tried to train them into a different mould. Wolz knew practically nothing about that end of the political scene, being a sailor; and even his cousin Helmut who was - Wolz felt convinced - in the Gestapo never talked of it. One just didn't.

His other cousins, Manfred in the Luftwaffe, and Siegfried in the Waffen SS, were out in the front line as he was, only they were in Russia. Wolz did not envy them.

At least, he believed Siegfried to be still in Russia. He was in SS Regiment Deutschland in SS Reich Division, newly named SS Das Reich. They'd had a horrific time of it, although Siegfried was, naturally, reluctant to spell it all out. They'd lost something like seven thousand men in wounded and killed and missing - the last a particularly unfortunate category of casualty. After that they'd lost another four thousand. And the fact remained, grim and brutal, that Moscow and Leningrad had not fallen - yet.

The last letters had sounded strained. Siegfried might be back in Germany, or even France, helping to reconstitute his regiment within what would amount to a new division. Wolz just hoped cousin Siegfried would make the most of his time. Somehow, the way things were going, Wolz didn't believe Siegfried had much time left in this world. And that sickened him.

After Baldur Wolz's father had been sunk in his U-boat right at the end of the last war – and by a damned lumbering, stupid, blind and criminal German minesweeper – Wolz's mother had not survived long. Wolz had gone to live with his Uncle Siegfried in the family schloss. His aunt made him welcome and treated him like another son. There were three sons of the family, Siegfried, Helmut and Manfred. And the daughter, Lisl.

When Wolz thought of Lisl, which he tried not to do, he experienced a pain in his insides that twisted him up. She was not for him, he had always felt that. Nothing had been said, by anyone involved, and now Lisl was in uniform and helping to win the war for Germany. Quite what she was doing Wolz did not know, and Uncle Siegfried had been particularly vague.

He lay with his eyes open. He could see Lisl as she had been when young. In that pretty white dress, her bare legs brown with the sun, racing them all down through the woods to the stream, yelling like banshees. The Wolzs knew the country around the schloss, the quick ways through the woods and along the contours of the hills. They'd been a gang of ruffians, bandits, and Wolz's feelings for Lisl had been so profound, so moving, that he could not face them.

Instead he had turned to jolly girls like Lottie and her friend Heidi, and all the others, romping the nights away and forcing Lisl from his mind.

And then Trudi von Hartstein had entered the picture. She'd lived in the neighbouring castle, for her widowed mother was the Baroness Elizabeth von Hartstein. Of course, titles even of so ancient and distinguished a form, meant little these days. Certainly, Trudi von Hartstein never acted in a stupid way about that.

If she acted stupidly or irrationally – even criminally – over other matters was a problem that bothered Wolz so much that he had been shattered to find himself almost relieved that Trudi had not contacted him at the schloss before he'd gone on to the Black Forest. There Gretchen and later Irmgard had taken up his time and thoughts.

Once, Wolz remembered, he'd sworn that, by God, if by some supreme stroke of good fortune he could ever marry Lisl, he would. Since then he had tacitly abandoned that idea. He had intended to ask Trudi to marry him. He'd even gone to see her with that firm intention. Twice. And on each occasion some fraught happening had interrupted mundane ideas of marriage. Happenings like burning cars and machine pistol fire in quiet German woods, and frantic dashes to the border, and secrets and whispered words and, finally, silence.

The last time he'd seen her she'd been in ghastly shape, dreadfully changed from the golden girl, all laughter and smiles and winningly artless ways she'd been when they'd first met. She'd been like a hunted animal, asking for money, skulking in the woods. And her friend had been shot by the Gestapo. And she'd been deathly afraid that Cousin Helmut might be at the schloss. No, Wolz was not relieved she hadn't tried to contact him.

He was chagrined, disturbed, and worried out of his mind about Trudi von Hartstein.

And, down in Italy, there was Iolanthe Fozazzaro, who was half Italian and half English, to intrude into his thoughts with surmises of what might be ...

He roused himself and made a round of the boat, which was a highly unpopular thing to do, and then climbed up to the bridge. The sun was declining. There was nothing fresh to report. He made arrangements for night steaming, and checked once more with Stuckl. He relieved the party in *Cotash* with a stronger detachment armed with machine pistols, and he sent over verbal instructions. He warned

Stuckl to be vigilant and to keep his eyes open. The men must watch for any attempt on the part of the British to take their ship back.

There were soldiers aboard, and soldiers at sea always posed problems.

They could easily do something damned stupid.

Wolz did not want to slip an eel into *Cotash* with Gerhardt aboard, and his IWO was in no shape to be moved yet.

Something in Gerhardt's grey-green face as they'd shipped him across reminded Wolz of the look in Trudi's face when he'd last seen her.

She'd worn an old leather coat cut short, and tight trousers, and a small felt cap pulled over her forehead. Her pale golden face was pallid, her eyes feverish. And under the coat a grey blouse that was a size too small for her outlined the shape of her breasts. He'd been tongue-tied, thick with longing and passion, standing like a loon knowing he could do nothing. They'd kissed. And then she'd gone, running into the shadows of the trees, gone with what money he had scraped together, borrowing on some trumped-up story from Siegfried and Manfred, gone.

What could she be about? She'd sworn that what she was doing could bring no harm to Germany, and he believed her.

So he'd romped with Mariza and Mimi and the others.

But Trudi, Trudi . . .

6

Sergeant Dave Brown touched the three tapes on his arm and wondered why he bothered. His khaki looked odd aboard a big ship, he knew that, didn't like ships, didn't trust them. Give him a field to plough, or the cows to milk, or any task to do with the farm back home in Upper Pennery Bottom in Wilts, and he'd know how to do it backwards. But he'd joined up and they'd put him in the Artillery and made him a sergeant because he could shout and he'd grasped the ins and outs of guns quickly. Well, he'd followed the guns at home, and he could put the contents of both barrels of a twelve bore where he wanted. He was a natural-born infantryman, but in the nature of square peggery and round holery they'd put him in the Artillery.

Locked with the gun crew down below he wondered how he could break out. If he could just get that rotten Jerry submarine in the sights of his three incher – no, she wouldn't depress. He'd have to use the six incher. He could get enough of the lads to follow him, he did not doubt. Just one good shot, smack in her guts, and that would be that.

Like a bird with her tail blown off over Denney woods . . .

Standing guard with an MP38 cradled across his stomach, Torpedo Mechaniker Hans Braun felt the movement of the big ship beneath him as a strange experience after the motion of a U-boat. He'd gone into the underwater arm of the Kriegsmarine – well, he wasn't really sure just how it had happened, but here he was and this was his job. He could hear the Englanders talking among themselves.

He wondered, not idly but with a sharp stab of apprehension, what he would do if they tried to escape.

He would have to shoot them, of course.

That seemed something monstrous, and yet accepted, a mere part of the routine of war. If the men in their khaki uniforms came running out, shouting, waving spanners to hit him over the head, he would have to point his MP38 and spray them with 9-mm bullets. He would have to shoot them.

One thing Hans Braun was sure of. He'd far rather be on the farm, a neat and tidy place just outside Langenneufnach, not too far from Augsburg. Far rather be there than here...

Despite the plans and apprehensions among captured and captors, the night passed uneventfully.

Or so it seemed on the surface of events.

Angus Macbright spent a great deal of blasphemous energy on the fuel pump. He had his gang stripping her right down. At least if he couldn't make that aul' fool Tom Antrobus stop one engine, the damned Jerries had.

Macbright saw that his lads were hard at it, finding the muck that was the source of the blockage, and clearing it out so that the whole unit shone like a new thrupenny bit.

Then he went into his cabin and stripped himself off and took a long hot shower. The muck simply rolled off him. He had a compact, muscular, gingery-haired body, and he made himself smell clean and sweet with soap and water.

Then he put on a clean white shirt and his second best trousers, smoothed his hair down, and opened the door of his cabin. The deck looked pale and ghostly. The passenger accommodation was conveniently located across the gangway on the other side. Macbright picked up his bottle of Scotch and whistled across the gangway and flattened out against the deckhouse like a weasel. He scratched on the door.

Miss Prothero opened the door, Macbright slid in, and the door closed.

She switched on the light. All the scuttles were blacked out.

Macbright smiled.

'Angus – another full bottle! You are – are –'

'If ye say naughty, lassie, I'll –'

She wore a peignoir of some distinction and age, and her pallidness was relieved and heightened by a flush. She was not quite forty-five years of age, and Angus Macbright was not her first man. The first was now a few bits and pieces of browned bone deeply sunk in the mud of a place called Passchendaele.

Macbright looked at her with lively appreciation.

She was thin, yes. But her breasts were full and round and without the hint of a sag. Her face pleased him. His own hard masculine roughness responded to her own strength which he recognised. That flush, now, staining along her cheekbones, making the pale face alive and warm – that was Agnes Prothero. He understood she was with some ministry or other and had been in the States as a P.A. to some big wig. Well, she was clearly somebody of importance to gain passage in wartime.

Now her eyes danced in lively anticipation as she opened the bottle and poured. The two glasses clinked.

'You'll what, Angus?'

'Take that fancy lace off, lassie, and you'll see.'

She did so.

Macbright laughed. She was just right, not too long in the tooth, juicy, and yet virginal in a way that he refused to let abash him. He was seriously considering Agnes Prothero, and he knew she was doing the same for him. They might be chalk and cheese. But they got on so well, in a kind of macabre ship-board romance out of dreams and moonlight, all teenage nonsense, that it might, just, work.

They drank and talked companionably for a space, sitting on the edge of her bunk swinging their toes. The Germans and their U-boat frightened Miss Prothero.

Macbright tried to reassure her.

'As soon as we've patched up their sick man, lassie, they'll be off. And good riddance.'

'Do you really believe that?'

'Of course.'

But he didn't.

They'd be lucky to get into an open lifeboat. Then they'd have to sail back to the States. He was sure, damned sure, that he'd be in the same lifeboat as Agnes Prothero.

Damned sure.

She leaned her head against his shoulder and put her hand, long and slim, inside his shirt. She could feel the ginger hairs. They made a shiver run through her body.

When he touched her, she bit her lip, and shivered more, and responded. Poor Alec - he'd gone off with his new uniform and the shining Sam Browne and the boyish smile and fair wavy hair, and there had been one letter and then the telegram to his parents. Nothing after that. Nothing except an aching void, dry and empty, until this gingery barbarian had, somehow, penetrated her automatic defences. She was glad he had. Wartime made one do strange things.

To think here she was, a serious professional career woman, with a boss to take care of, a department to run, letting a man run his hands over her body, fondle her breasts, letting him kiss her, letting him - she lay back with a gasp and Macbright rolled over. Well, if they could not enjoy themselves during a situation like this - who could?

T. R. Antrobus rang down to the engine room to find out how the repairs were coming along.

The third engineer told him they were working as fast as they could, and that the pump ought to be back together by the morning watch.

'Jumph!' said T. R. Antrobus, and bit down on his bulldog. He did not ask to speak to his Chief Engineer.

If that fool Macbright, an escapee from the Gorbals or some heathen precinct of a similar nature, didn't think that the master knew what he was up to, then Macbright was all kinds of idiot. And as for Miss Prothero, the very sight of her parasol made a haze swim over Tom Antrobus's eyes.

At least, she wore lavender water and not perfume. There was that to be said for her.

He wondered who was trying to get at Mary Parson. If it was any of his crew, any of his three cadets, or one of his officers, he'd keelhaul the bugger. Maybe it was that snooty Lieutenant Commander. Well, T. R. Antrobus wished them bad cess, for Mary Parson was something special in his eyes. He could see quite clearly the difference between Mary Parson and Miss Prothero. The difference accounted for his actions. He was not much aware of his own motives. But he knew that he was right.

He fretted over what the morrow might bring.

There was little chance that *Cotash* would not be sunk.

He'd grieve for his ship. His duty would be to ensure there were no casualties, or as few as possible. By proper management the boats could be lowered and they could sail back to the States. He'd have the hide off anyone who misbehaved. But during that night T. R. Antrobus spent many hours in mental agony. He did not think there was much chance of taking his ship back from the Nazis. No doubt he'd try. No doubt he would and no doubt somebody would be killed. This was a decision he would have to take, and it was a decision of life and death he could wish to be without.

A ship at sea is never truly silent, and idling along though she was, *Cotash* still breathed with the sounds of her calling. But all else in the ship lay ghostly, eerie, silent with an unaccustomed hollowness of feeling. Lightless and yet alive, she moved slowly through the water. Her gangways and corridors, her deck, seemed peopled with ghosts.

And, pacing her, watching, ready to destroy, the lean shark shape of the U-boat prowled like a guardian demon.

Despite all the fun and games, with Gretchen as with anyone else, Baldur Wolz persisted in regarding this holiday period in the Black Forest hotel as a fallow period. He had completed a phase of his life, his operational career could stand the minutest inspection, with the single exception of the abortive attack on Barca harbour. And that had been in the end the fault of inadequate intelligence information.

He had proved himself a capable, even a dashing, U-boat commander. He wore the Iron Cross, First and Second Class. He wore the U-boat badge, and wound badges, and various bits and pieces of metal and coloured ribbons. He wore the Narvik Shield - on dress uniform only. These adornments had to be worn with some discretion. He had sunk a fair amount of tonnage. He was now genuinely in the hunt for his one hundred thousand tons. Perhaps, then, he might be awarded the Knights Cross to the Iron Cross.

Tumbling Gretchen on the sheepskin rug before the log fire seemed to him far more important than bits of metal and coloured ribbons.

As he stroked the valley between her breasts, watching the flicker of the firelight casting dancing shadows from her nipples, and kissing her every now and again, just lying comfortably together gathering strength, he reflected that all this was far more important, all, perhaps, except for one over-riding demand in his life.

Perhaps ... Only perhaps.

The one thing he hungered, craved, demanded, must have, was command of an operational U-boat.

That, to Baldur Wolz, one of the Grey Wolves, the man they called the Sea Wolf, that was the drug he craved.

Gretchen sat up, slender and yet full, and bit his ear.

'Oh!'

'Did I tell you Irmgard is visiting?'

'No.'

'Well, she is. And you must behave and be nice to her.'

Wolz put on a U-boatman's leer. He reached his hand down to her thighs and tingled his fingertips along. She arched back. 'Nice like this?' said Baldur Wolz, laughing.

And she shook him.

'We-ell - just wait and see.'

His hand stopped, and spread, pressing into her flesh.

'Perhaps,' he said, and his laugh changed to a little uncertain frown of anticipation. 'I ought to telegraph some friends of mine – if they have leave, which I doubt.'

'No, Baldur. Irmgard and I – no, I think it best not to.'

'Very well.'

She began to play with him, casually, aware they were both waiting. 'Tell me, Baldur, is it really true that you U-boatmen wear perfume?'

He lay back, his hand trailing along warm skin.

'Some of the fellows do, yes. I suppose you get used to how the boat smells after a time. And some of the lads feel that scent only makes it worse. We're a pretty sweaty bunch, though –'

'Tell me. What's it like?'

He did not automatically say, as he might have done a year ago, 'No, that's quite impossible.' Instead, he said, 'Not much to tell. We're cooped up in a steel tube. Lots of bits and pieces of metal to bang your head on. And, of course, it does smell unless we can ventilate frequently.'

'And the enemy?'

'Them!'

How could he tell her of the real conditions in a U-boat? He just couldn't. The stench of fear as the wabos tumbled down. The awful concussions as they exploded. The lash of the enemy's underwater detection apparatus, whipping across the hull, knocking to come in ... The closeness of it all, the lack of breath, the fear, the fear ... No, he couldn't tell her that.

'There are some clever captains in the enemy navy now. But we keep ahead of them.'

'Irmgard knew a nice young man, Oberleutnant Muller, who was in U-boats. She hasn't seen him lately. He was just reported missing in action.'

Wolz sat up. He looked fierce. He wasn't going to have this. He wasn't on survivor's leave in the Black Forest, and romping with a girl, to talk about U-boats.

He believed in doing.

'You have had two husbands, you told me, Gretchen.'

She looked into his face where the firelight set ruddy planes and hollowed shadows. She was startled by his tone.

'Yes?'

'One was in the Luftwaffe and the other in the Heer, and they are both dead. It's not only U-boats that get you killed.'

'Oh, Baldur!'

And, so you see, he said bitterly to himself as she caught his head and imprisoned it between her breasts, so you see. Here was another woman who had penetrated his secret.

Not that, in the U-boat arm, it was much of a secret anyway.

Lieutenant Commander Hugh Chalfont, RN, had slept little during the night. With first light he was on deck and leaning on the rail brooding on the ugly shape of the U-boat running with such infernal cheek alongside.

Chalfont wanted to do one thing.

He wanted to sink that U-boat.

He could feel some brotherly understanding for the plight of her skipper. The German officer who'd been brought aboard *Cotash* was an uncomfortable reminder to Chalfont. He, himself, had been taken off HMS *Whippet* with an appendix misbehaving itself and rushed to hospital. He supposed he'd been fortunate that it had happened at the western edge of the Big Pond, as the Yanks called the Atlantic. He'd had first class medical attention. And now, convalescing, for he'd been really down after the op, he was on his way home to resume sea duty. He wondered if he'd get *Whippet* back. He doubted it. Probably they'd give him command of a Flower, or perhaps a sloop – it all depended on chance, he supposed.

So, now, a big raw-boned man with an ugly face and unshaven chin, he glowered down on the U-boat.

Captain T. R. Antrobus, puffing his foul pipe, walked across to join the navy man.

'Morning, captain.'

'Morning, commander.' Antrobus nodded. 'If we could –'

'Yes.'

'Not much chance, though.'

'I suppose that efficient Jerry officer took the keys to the armoury?'

'He did that.' Antrobus puffed and the morning air took on a haze around his head. 'But I've a revolver in my cabin they don't know about.'

'Well,' said Lieutenant Commander Hugh Chalfont. 'That's a start.'

Kapitänleutnant Baldur Wolz stared at the message flimsy. The Enigma had chunked out the answer to the riddle contained in the coded signal. His report to BdU had been received with reserve; but with less criticism than he had expected.

His explanation that he would refuel and re-provision before sinking *Cotash* received affirmation. Dönitz was an old U-boatman himself. He understood that a submarine patrol was not a question of dashing about the high seas loosing off torpedoes and sinking ship after ship. That was the romance of it. The practicality was the long patient stalk, the positioning and then the loosing. A hit was an achievement. Until they were back in among the convoys, that would be the way of it now. So that a few days lost, with a certain sinking at their end, and the recuperation of a fine and valuable U-boat First Watch Officer, were not really wasted.

Wolz crumpled the flimsy in his hand.

He would take everything he wanted from *Cotash* and spare nothing. Anything he did not take would go down fathoms deep, lost for ever.

In his bones he knew that the English over there were planning mischief.

He knew that, had the positions been reversed, he would be actively planning to take back the ship and, if possible, sink the cheeky U-boat who had captured her.

That was so certain as not to need worry. The worry was how to stop the English, beat them into sense, stop any attempt at retaking the ship before he had finished his business with her. That was the problem facing him in the immediate present and until Fritz Gerhardt could be brought back to U-451.

7

The hands sported on the forecasing. They were stripped naked and they had a hose connected up and were squirting water around, splashing and shouting, completely involved in horseplay that took them out of the steely confines of the boat.

Wolz, his white cap cover gleaming in the sunshine, looked on from the bridge.

He did not smile. This was so weird a development in the underwater war at sea that he only half-believed it.

No doubt of it. He'd taken *Cotash* and U-451 down on a course out of any regular sealanes, and, should a patrolling aircraft appear - an eventuality here so unlikely as to be virtually ignored - the men could swim for it if they didn't get down the hatches in time. *Cotash* herself would provide so splendid a cover that Wolz had no doubts of the successful outcome.

Stuckl aboard *Cotash* could hook the men out of the sea. Proper signals could be made. And the aeroplane would fly off and U-451 would resurface.

The chance of a patrolling destroyer finding them was low. But, if one did so chance upon them, the arrangements would be somewhat different. The lookouts, for all the skylarking going on, stuck rigidly to their quadrants. If one of them failed to spot the dot of an approaching ship, he'd be for so high a jump he'd squeak - if he lived.

After that, if Stuckl in *Cotash* couldn't manage to convince the inquisitive destroyer that the vessel was in no trouble and was proceeding normally, U-451, lurking under the massive hull, would slap a couple of eels in. Set on shallow, they'd rip the destroyer to pieces.

Come to think of it, that might be quite worth doing.

BdU had signalled that a milch cow would be in the rendezvous area soon, and Wolz could restock with torpedoes from her. He would not need oil. He was taking that from MV *Cotash*'s bunkers.

Baldur Wolz kept up to date with all the news coming in. He did rounds. He made sure his command was in perfect shape – give or take the problems with the diesel and a few minor irritants the Chief was working on. He had the two midshipmen shoot the sun at midday, and generally kept their noses to the grindstone. Gerhardt was progressing satisfactorily, and the doctor, under some inquisitive questioning, half-promised that the IWO might be moved back to U-451 on the morrow. They'd take every precaution with Gerhardt, and the Sanitätsobermaat would be told very thoroughly just what was required of him in Gerhardt's care and attention after the op. Very thoroughly.

A light began to blink rapidly from the bridge wing of MV *Cotash*.

The signalman on the bridge of U-451 acknowledged with his own lamp and began to take down the incoming signal from the German signalman in the English ship. As he wrote so Wolz read off the rapid morse.

From the higher vantage point of the ship an observation of the horizon would extend further. The lookouts up there had spotted a smudge of smoke that, whilst it would certainly be a ship, might be a tanker, a freighter, a destroyer or even a battleship.

Wolz ordered action stations, and the forecasing cleared of naked men as though it had begun to snow.

'Send to Leutnant Stuckl,' Wolz told the signalman. 'Keep control. We shall not be gone long. Do not hesitate to shoot to maintain order and your authority. Sign it Wolz, U-451.'

'Very good!'

The IIWO had slept during the night, and he had two reliable warrant officers with him. Wolz would miss them if he had to carry out an attack; but they could not be in two places at once.

He sent the watch below, gave a last look around, waved to the slab-sided hull and bridge of MV *Cotash*, and then dropped down the ladder. He slammed the lid and turned the wheel.

Diving the boat in these conditions was just a little more difficult. The hands had to do more than usual. Wolz himself chipped in. His own brand of leadership showed itself as U-451 slid below without fuss, everything going smoothly.

'Take us down to twenty metres, Chief.'

'Very good.'

The sunlight through the water struck with a diffused and greenish tint through the eyepiece of the scope. U-boatmen called the periscope the *spargel*, asparagus, and now Wolz jockeyed U-451 into position beneath *Cotash*. He hung there, pacing the ship, listening to the sounds reaching him through the water levels.

Presently the hydrophone operator reported that he could distinguish the distant sounds of screws through the mush of *Cotash*. He was doing a first class job. The difficulty of obtaining accurate results under these conditions was well nigh insuperable; but German underwater listening equipment was superb, far superior to anything the Allies employed.

'Steady on bearing, skipper. He's heading right for us.'

'Then he is in for a surprise.'

Someone laughed.

That was not so strange a sound in a U-boat; but it did sound more than a little odd.

This enforced period of idleness had infected the crew. They had absolute confidence in their skipper. They called Wolz 'Daddy' among themselves, and that always heartened the commander of a U-boat.

They expected him to perform miracles.

To look at they were a bearded, sweaty, scruffy bunch.

They wore old sweaters and short monkey jackets. They had sidecaps perched on their heads, the eagle and the national cockade flaunting; they wore regulation naval caps; they wore sneakers for ease of movement in a boat. Practically no one wore any rings on any fingers. Rings had a habit of becoming caught on projections and, being dragged away, of taking with them the fingers inside them. They were men living on borrowed time.

When they carried out their duties they moved with quick frenetic movements, turning wheels, pulling levers, checking dials, and every sudden action vividly conveyed a sense of galvanic energy. The scene inside a U-boat might resemble that in a seventh hell; but every man knew what he was doing and did it with every gram of his willpower.

Wolz felt the sense of elation. He had a good crew, although he still had to work on the raw hands, and they might be depleted by the party left in *Cotash*; he had no doubt that they would serve both him and U-451 well.

When the right moment arrived he would come gently to periscope depth and blow this noseyparker right out of the water. The end would be sudden and decisive. Then he could get back to seeing about taking Gerhardt off and resuming his interrupted patrol.

But, first, he had a ship to sink . . .

'The bastard's submerging,' observed Lieutenant Commander Chalfont.

'And I could wish he never comes up again.'

T. R. Antrobus took his bulldog from his mouth, tamped the bowl with a blackened thumb. 'But he's up to mischief.'

Chalfont nodded towards the plume of smoke on the horizon.

'That's what's caused this, no doubt of it. Now if that is a destroyer –'

'If!'

Both men stood at the rail, aware of the armed German guard standing with ready machine pistol at their backs.

The Germans had tight control of *Cotash*. Even Angus Macbright in his own engine room was kept under the kind of surveillance they never experienced in the Barlinnie. There were not too many Nazis aboard; but they were stationed at key points.

Chalfont rubbed his bristly chin. He was determined to grow a full set before he reached England.

'Now if we could signal her —'

'If she's a destroyer –'

'Yes.'

'Along with that revolver of mine there's a signalling lamp –'

'Capital!' Chalfont looked around casually. As far as he was aware the Jerries did not speak English; but looks of pleasure on the faces of their captives must arouse suspicion. 'Right. Well, we'll just have to make time for me to signal. Agreed?'

Antrobus's initial, soured, view of Chalfont as 'that snooty Lieutenant Commander' had undergone substantial revision since the ship had been taken over. The navy man looked and sounded determined in his offhand way.

Maybe, just maybe, they could signal the approaching vessel. If she was a warship or another merchantman, it was their duty to warn her.

'Right,' said Tom Antrobus. 'We have to make a diversion.'

'I'll leave that to you. Point me in the direction of your revolver and the lamp – and I'll make the signal.'

Geschutz-Führer, Einzel-geschutz, Otto Meyer had worked in a fish and chip shop in Hull for over five years. Sometimes he still could smell the aroma of fish and chips in his nostrils. Then he'd gone back to Hamburg and had found himself in the Kriegsmarine, and in the U-boat arm, with a red embroidered badge on his arm saying he was a single-gun gun pointer. His English was thick, unpretty and of the basic kind.

As Leutnant zur See Franz Stuckl shoved the muzzle of his Walther P38 into the guts of First Officer James Ogilvie, Otto Meyer translated.

'You are to make the correct signals. If you don't –' Meyer paused to get it right, and then said, 'Shot. You are to be shot.'

'Goddam you,' said Ogilvie. He was tall and thin and he towered cadaverously over the chunky Meyer.

Stuckl understood what the skinny Englishman was saying. The fellow looked like a bean pole. He jabbed the automatic in harder.

'You will do as you are told,' said Meyer, on the heels of Stuckl's harsh words.

If Ogilvie didn't want his stomach shot past his backbone there was nothing else he could do but obey. He gave his orders in a weary voice.

'Make the correct signals. We don't want to get ourselves killed.'

Stuckl smiled as Meyer reported what the Englishman had said. It was all going to be all right. He was very glad that Daddy hadn't sent that maniac of a Fahnrich, Ulrich Rudhart, over to *Cotash*. Because U-451 was short-handed now a strong party was away from the boat, Rudhart had been let out and returned to duty. He was a chastened young man. Wolz could have his skin off if he liked. The crew would have gleefully and vengefully assisted. Taking a pot shot at the skipper! But Rudhart was needed in U-451, and Stuckl was glad the maniac was not here with him.

He said to Meyer, 'Go down and tell the English captain I want him up here on the bridge. Move.'

'Very good!'

Cotash was a fine large ship. Stuckl's men had rounded up the English and were holding them locked up. The quicker all this was over and Fritz was back aboard U-451 the better. Stuckl held his automatic in his hand all the time now and mindful of Wolz's orders was prepared to use it.

*

The signalling lamp was not an Aldiss pattern; but it was relatively new and looked efficient. Chalfont hefted the thing in the captain's cabin. He looked down at the open drawer, the key to which had been taken from an inside pocket of Antrobus's jacket. The revolver was large, clumsy, oiled, and looked as though it had been used at the Siege of Mafeking. He decided to leave it where it was.

This would be a job for stealth and cunning, not brute force and ignorance.

He shut the drawer and locked it and stowed the key away deep among the loose change in his trouser pocket.

If the Jerries suddenly took it into their square heads to come down to the captain's cabin, things could turn nasty.

He needed a perch out of the way, on the same side of the ship as the approaching vessel and out of direct observation of any German sentry. He felt a strange fluttery feeling, high up in his stomach, just under his breast bone. He knew what fear was - very few men who sailed in escorts across the Atlantic did not know what fear was like - and this feeling was odd and different.

He shook his head, banished the cageful of birds in his guts, took up the lamp and crossed to the cabin door.

A swift look out showed the corridor to be empty. Further along lay the cabins of the rest of the deck officers, those of the engineering personnel next, and opposite to them the cabins of the passengers. He held the lamp down at his side and walked swiftly and quietly. He reached the door he wanted and without knocking opened it and went into the cabin beyond.

Mary Parson swung about in the centre of the cabin.

She wore a short-sleeved pale blue frock, with narrow white lace at elbows and neck. Her face was very pale. She put a hand to her throat, staring at Hugh Chalfont with anticipatory dread.

'It's all right, Mary. Keep calm. I have to –'

'What's happened? Hugh - tell me, what is it?'

She looked like a Sunday School teacher in that dress and

the fawn sensible shoes that did not match. She wore no jewellery. Her brown hair was combed; but it looked, somehow, disarranged. She was very frightened.

He tried to reassure her.

'There's no need to be frightened. Nothing's happened.'

'But you look so – so grim.'

He crossed to the scuttle and drew the curtain. He looked out. The smoke of the oncoming vessel was now clearly visible even from this low vantage point, and he calculated he had very little time left to make this girl do as he wanted.

'The Jerries made a list of all the crew and passengers.' He faced her, and try as he might he could not get the tenseness out of his voice, the drawn lines out of his face. He couldn't smile. 'I need five minutes alone. When they round us up, Mary, you just go along like a good girl. Say nothing. Just say you haven't seen me if they ask. Do you understand?'

She put a hand to her hair. Her eyes regarded him more with unease now than fear. She swallowed.

'What are you going to do?'

'You don't have to worry about that. These Jerries have behaved properly so far. They are rotten U-boatmen, and my job is to sink them. But this is – different.'

'Hugh! I'm – I'm –'

He put the lamp down and reached for her. He had never touched her before. She gripped him with arms that tightened in fear and he gasped.

'Mary! Look – it will be all right.'

'Suppose they –'

'They won't. Once they get their officer back into their submarine they'll be off.'

'And then –'

He cursed himself for a babbling fool, and then he stopped that nonsense. Everyone aboard knew the Jerries would sink them once they'd got what they came for. Then would be the time for the kind of strong action he and Antrobus had discussed. If this approaching vessel was a warship, then she might just be the joker in the pack . . .

He gave her a hug, then released her and stepped back. She was reluctant to let him go.

'I'm going to hide.' He picked up the lamp. 'Now, remember. Just act normally. And you haven't seen me.'

A hard knock rapped on the door and a heavy voice called out in German.

Clutching his lamp, Chalfont dived under the bunk and hauled the blankets down. He curled up. Perhaps he *ought* to have brought that damned great revolver, after all . . .

Torpedo Mechaniker Hans Braun knocked again and then called out as old Fishanchips Meyer had instructed.

'Kom out pleez.'

The door opened and the girl appeared. Braun jerked the muzzle of his machine pistol.

That potent international language could not be misunderstood.

Meekly, Mary Parson went along to join Miss Prothero and the other passengers as they were herded out and into the lounge where a careful German eye could be kept upon them.

In Mary Parson's cabin Chalfont crawled out from under the bunk and eased over to the door. He locked it. Then he crossed to the scuttle and looked out. The smoke was now much closer, and there was a great deal less of it. Had he been in command of the ship out there he'd have been on the pipe to the Chief in the engineroom blistering him with reprimands about making so much damn smoke. The blackness of the smoke lightened into a grey and wisped. He could now just about make out a darkness beneath that would be the hull; but a few more minutes must elapse before he could start to signal.

He lifted the lamp and made sure it was working correctly.

Then he aimed it through the scuttle and waited, fingers on the trigger, ready.

8

'Find him!' said Oberleutnant zur See Franz Stuckl. 'Find him. If you have to shoot, shoot! *Move*!'

'Very good!'

The party of hands from U-451 scattered about the vast areas of MV *Cotash* in search of the elusive passenger.

Stuckl's automatic covered T. R. Antrobus and the bridge watch. He'd shot men before, and he'd shoot this lot if he had to. Daddy would not welcome a disaster as a result of Stuckl's inefficiency.

Down in U-451 Wolz brought her gently to fourteen metres on the blind side of the ship. Running like this with the wash of *Cotash* to contend with, driving along with the rudders angled to compensate, called for consummate steering.

The Chief held her level and true, and the steuermann held her straight.

Gingerly, Wolz upped the scope and peered cautiously around. On one flank only the tall, blackish, rust-streaked grey-speckled side of the ship towered up. On the other the tops of the rippling waves showed sea flowing past, and the tall sky sloping above. He could not see the on-coming ship. Well, he'd see her when she was close enough.

'Down periscope.'

'Down periscope.'

The spargel hissed down into the well.

He wished he knew what was going on in *Cotash*. Anything could be happening. Stuckl was a hard man. He'd come to U-boats from the army, one of the shufflings to make better use of manpower, and he'd been through the mill. He was shaping up, and if he didn't get himself killed he would one day command one of the fine new boats the German yards were building as fast as they could.

That background would be of help now in controlling the fractious crew in the English ship. That they'd make some attempt to signal was without question. All Baldur Wolz needed was a good shot, and the problem would be solved.

Cautiously, as befitted a U-boat commander, he edged U-451 along, pacing the ship at his side. The moment the enemy vessel came into his sights – one good shot. That was all . . .

Lieutenant Commander Rufus K. Barnum came up onto his bridge and looked through the glasses at the ship some distance ahead. The sea was calm, the sky blue and high, with only a few clouds. The bridge watch appeared to be on their toes, and Barnum felt halfway happy with them. Just give his ship's company a few more weeks of hard training, of keeping their noses to it, and they might shape up.

As for his ship – USS *Ackermann* had been launched in 1934 and was a fine fast destroyer and he'd been overjoyed to gain command. She was probably a trifle over-gunned, with five 5-inch guns and with eight 21-inch torpedo tubes on only one thousand three hundred and fifty tons displacement. But he intended to make her a top line ship. If the bows did fall off in bad weather, well, she'd be rebuilt and this time they'd plan differently.

'Nothing from her, sir,' reported his exec, Lieutenant Johannsen; unnecessarily, in Barnum's view. Had there been a signal from the ship he'd have known about it by now.

The turbines thrummed deep in the ship, thrilling up through the decks and vibrating Barnum's ankle bones. He was a big man, florid, handsome, and he never did like leaving Mamie at home with the kids. But now there was a shooting war on, the quicker he worked *Ackermann* up into a fighting unit of the navy the better. He would have preferred to be in the Pacific and knocking hell out of the

Nips; as it was here he was in the Atlantic.

He stared ahead. The ship up there remained silent.

This was no business of his, of course. That vessel ahead was more than likely on her proper pursuits. But she could be a Nazi blockade runner, or supply ship. The Kraut U-boats had been wreaking a dreadful havoc, and they'd most likely have supply ships at sea.

If she was, then Barnum would be grateful for all five of his five inchers. She'd most likely have a few 5.9s tucked away in dummy deckhouses.

This was all a fantasy, of course. But it was not impossible.

He had to think of every eventuality.

'Left standard rudder. Steer course one-two-eight.'

The quartermaster repeated. 'Left standard rudder. Course one-two-eight.'

Ackermann began to turn as her rudder bit.

Just in case, Barnum told himself, just in case. He'd cross this vessel's stern, signalling by lamp before he passed out of her bridge view. That way if she was some damned Kraut battlewagon disguised as a motor vessel he'd be in range of only one or two of her concealed guns. He didn't believe any of this; but it was all good training.

If he ranged up alongside she could get a good crack at him and might do enough damage on that first strike to cripple him. Better safe than sorry.

Moments later the quartermaster sang out.

'Steady on course one-two-eight.'

'Very well,' said Barnum, and put the glasses to his eyes again.

Now he could see her more clearly. She flew the British Red Ensign and was a fine large modern passenger cargo liner. The exec was leafing through the book to make an early identification. Barnum began to compose a short and succinct message. Really, he had little business doing this; but anything to put something different into the training routine was welcome.

The bell rang and the signalman answered, speaking in hushed yet clipped tones down the pipe.

Barnum took no notice.

The quartermaster kept his eyes on the compass repeater.

Johannsen came across with a clipboard. The paper flicked in the wind of their passage.

'Message, sir –'

Barnum barely glanced at the Eastern Sea Frontier sending coding; the message itself leaped out at him.

'Submarine sighting,' he read. He took a breath. This message would not have been sent to a boat still in training had not the sighting been firm, and his presence necessary. The position given was less than a hundred miles north of east. He handed the clipboard back.

'Left full rudder. Steer course zero-eight-five.'

The quartermaster, a very old hand, picked up the tone of voice. He slapped out his repeat. 'Left full rudder. Course zero-eight-five.'

'All engines ahead flank speed. Make turns for twenty-five knots.'

'All engines ahead flank speed. Make turns for twenty-five knots.'

He crossed to the pipe to the chart room below.

The boat was leaning over as she turned, and he found himself leaning with her in the old practised way.

The course to the point of contact would be traced by the navigator. They'd come roaring up and begin a search and, here Barnum crossed his fingers, if the sonar did not pack up on them they'd get a pip and pick up the U-boat. Then, if the depth charges went down right they'd make their first kill of the war.

That, on a training cruise, would be something!

'Steady on course zero-eight-five.'

'Very well.'

Ackermann began to pulse with power. White water began to rise and break away from her sharp bows in two curving wings. She thrashed along. Barnum wondered just how fast he dared push her. The engine room personnel were keen to go; but they were new, raw. If he blew it now, he might never get another chance.

Four hours ahead lay a meeting with a U-boat, if he was lucky. If he could squeeze a few more knots out of her, and she'd been built to make thirty-six and a half knots, he could cut that time meaningfully.

Best thing was to have a word with the Chief ...

The signalman started to clack his lamp and Barnum looked up quickly. The talker waited. Then the shutters stilled. *Ackermann* was now almost stern on and the angles fined down.

'Well?'

'They tried to send a signal, sir –'

'Tried?'

'Very odd, sir.' He was a youngish lad, with gingery hair and a spotty face. He had, Barnum recalled, been hopelessly seasick for the first five days. Now he still looked green.

'Could you read any of it?'

Barnum had no intention whatsoever of turning back just so this message could be taken in.

'Not much sir. Just the words U-boat, and beware – but the message stopped –'

'When we passed out of view?'

'No, sir. Just before.'

'Well,' said Barnum. 'We're off to get his U-boat for him. Nice of him to wish us well, though.'

USS *Ackermann,* roaring with power, foamed along towards the reported contact, and very soon MV *Cotash* was a mere dot upon the sea. And soon after that she vanished over the horizon rim.

Staring out of the port, fingers nervously tapping at the trigger of the signalling lamp, Hugh Chalfont saw the smudge of thinning smoke start to change bearing. It was no longer aimed directly at him. The smoke began to move aft.

He understood at once what was going on, what the

skipper in the approaching vessel was thinking and the reasons for his change of course.

Lieutenant Commander Hugh Chalftont, RN, knew he would be doing just the same. He might have chosen to cross ahead rather than astern. That would have taken longer with the courses as they were; it would have been safer.

He gripped the handle of the signalling lamp and swung away from the scuttle.

He would just damn well have to work his own way aft and find another spot to signal from. And it wouldn't be a nice cosy cabin with the faint smell of perfume, and a scrap of lace and silk hanging out of a half-closed drawer. He crossed to the door and listened. The sounds of the ship flowed over him, heard and sorted and ignored. He could hear nothing untoward. He pulled the door open and peeked out. The corridor was empty.

Walking with a swing, purposeful, he started aft.

'He has to be somewhere!' Franz Stuckl put an edge to his voice. 'Search every cabin again. You, Muller, go forward. You, Braun, go aft. Check everywhere, every scuttle, every hiding place where he can signal from.'

There was no need to spell it out.

Stuckl and all the German boarding party knew that was the reason the English naval officer had vanished. He was going to signal to the oncoming ship. Stuckl sweated. Wolz would not care for that at all.

'It won't do you any good, you know,' said T. R. Antrobus as the spate of harsh German words dried. What they were saying in their barbarous tongue meant nothing; what they meant was obvious.

Stuckl ignored the master. He didn't even bother to get Meyer to translate. The hands called the man from Hamburg Fishanchips Meyer. Stuckl would cut all these Englanders up into fish and chips if they outwitted him. The mad English naval officer had to be found ...

Torpedo Mechaniker Hans Braun moved carefully along

the upper deck. The deckhouses had been searched and were being searched again. He could imagine his comrades pulling the pretty clothes out of that pretty girl's cabin to see if the Englander was hiding behind a woman's petticoats. He had caught the aft deck. Well, he couldn't see any sign of anyone, and off the starboard quarter the smoke was drifting up from the approaching vessel.

He would reach the stern in time to see if the Englander was there before the ship out there contacted them. She was a destroyer, that was clear, an Amerikaner, lean and low and looking remarkably like a good German destroyer. He checked in a lifeboat and then clattered down the ladder and went on aft. Stuckl sent Georg to look out for the other side, and Braun felt more comfortable with a comrade.

He held the MP38 across his waist.

The sun cast a jumble of shadows across the deck. He thought he glimpsed movement near the stern. He moved forward more purposefully, quietly, and he eased the machine pistol forward so that it snouted ahead of him.

He lost sight of the destroyer beyond the small deck house aft. He and Georg met there, quietly. Each man shook his head. Then Georg, a heavy-set man with very dark hair, nodded his head up. He put his left hand on the rail of the short ladder leading to the roof of the deckhouse.

Whispering, Braun said, 'Careful the Amerikaners don't see you.'

Georg nodded again and started up the ladder.

Cautiously, Hans Braun pushed the door open and went inside. This was a deckhouse used by the hands and even as he caught the fusty smell he saw by the light of the far scuttles a form moving. It was just a silhouette against the row of ports.

Unmistakably, loud and clattering, the sound of a signal lamp cut through the deckhouse.

Hans Braun was keyed up, tense, nervous, imagining all kinds of horrors. He was barely conscious of quite what he was doing. The machine pistol seemed to shoot itself.

Certainly, he had no recollection of pressing the trigger.

The splatter of bullets began and stopped.

In the instant that Braun realised he was shooting he snatched his right hand away from the machine pistol. It swung on its strap about his neck.

For Lieutenant Commander Hugh Chalfont, RN, the day ended.

He dropped the signal lamp. He'd got off a brief warning that there was a U-boat and for the destroyer to beware and then he felt a blow, a series of heavy blows, in his back.

He fell. He fell down and sprawled on his face and the blood began to ooze from his back. The stink of burnt gunpowder hung in the deckhouse. And Hans Braun looked down in horror upon his handiwork.

9

Hugh Chalfont was buried at sea with all due formality and protocol. They even found a White Ensign to cover his sheeted body. There was a proper service, and a great deal of saluting. Everything that had to be done was done, Wolz saw to that.

As for the hysterical outbursts of some of the English passengers, they had to be disregarded.

Chalfont was a serving naval officer. He had been unfortunately killed during an act of war. Absolutely no blame could attach to Torpedo Mechaniker Hans Braun.

As for Braun - he was profoundly impressed by the enormity of what he had done. Wolz told the Sanitätsobermaat to give him a sedative and Braun was relieved of duty for his next watch.

After that, he would be back on duty bright and chipper, or the commander would have his skin off.

All the same, Baldur Wolz would have a few quiet words with him, and ensure that Braun suffered no remorse. Duty was a funny old animal. Wolz was not prepared to pass judgement on Braun's actions. Had he been there, in the sudden gloom of the aft deckhouse, aware that a dangerous enemy officer was aboard, and seen the dark figure, and heard the signalling lamp, knowing an American destroyer was steaming only a short distance away - would he have challenged first, before shooting?

Could he be sure he would have done? Perhaps a challenge would have brought a pistol shot. The Englishman was unarmed; but Braun was not to know that.

All in all, Wolz decided, it was best to treat the incident as just another unhappy episode of total world war. He did not like that; but it was done and over, and no good would come of making Braun suffer any more.

Anyway, the Yankee had sheered off and gone like a bat out of hell towards the east. There'd been a trifle of north in his heading. Wolz supposed he'd been called away to chase U-boats.

During the second dog watch he received the message for which he had been waiting. Fritz Gerhardt was recovering well, and the doctor thought he could be moved on the morrow, probably in the forenoon watch. This pleased Wolz. Now perhaps he could get about his business in these waters.

He went down to his cabin and pulled the green curtain across. He was tired. Well, that was a normal everyday affair when he was at sea. He ought, really, to try to snatch a few hours sleep. There would be much to do tomorrow. He grappled with the details, sorting through priorities in his mind, arranging the order in which certain acts must be done. Yes, yes that would be the way of it.

There should be no fuss, no great emotional boiling over. That could lead to trouble. He'd have the British off their ship and safely out of it in their boats. Yes.

He called the cox'n and gave him his orders, which amounted only to running a taut boat and keeping the lookouts' eyes open.

'Call me – you know, cox'n.'

'Yes, sir. I know. Very good!'

Wolz lay on his bunk and closed his eyes and he saw Cousin Siegfried, as clear as clear, in his field grey SS uniform, smiling at him. Marlene was draped on his arm, svelte and voluptuous and her face smooth and unlined. Wolz smiled. He was pleased that Siegfried and Marlene had made it up.

They'd had a real party then! Siegfried had been overjoyed that he'd been assigned to training and bringing up to field competence a new detachment for his battalion. He'd mentioned old Trojer Ehrlacher, who'd been wounded – Siegfried did not say where, either on Ehrlacher's anatomy or in Russia – and was livid that he was being sent to a camp as part of a guard detail. A few wounded SS before return to duty were assigned as guards to the work camps where criminals were held. Siegfried said that he knew very little about that side of operations, having seen action in the Waffen SS. Siegfried had continued to hold his smile as he mentioned this; but Wolz knew his cousin well enough and saw quite clearly that Siegfried was not entirely at ease. Something was troubling him. But he roared out the old songs and joined in with the fun and games rampaging in the schloss, and then he was gone. Marlene was back in Berlin. And Wolz was again at a loose end.

He almost packed up and went back to the Black Forest; Irmgard – well, he wouldn't forget *her* in a hurry!

And he pestered BdU for a command.

But, all the same, something was bothering Cousin Siegfried and Wolz did not know what it was.

Looking back, Baldur Wolz wondered if he should curse fate that he hadn't gone back to the Black Forest hotel. His pay would have stretched, just. But, on the other hand, he knew only too well that he could never wish that he had. Not when what happened had happened, when it was too late to alter a jot or tittle of it . . .

Uncle Siegfried, who usually took himself off somewhere about business when his SS son entertained in the schloss, returned. He was brimful of energy. This heartened Wolz. The munitions business, quite clearly, was booming; but there were all manner of shortages to contend with.

Uncle Siegfried poo-poohed most of them.

He cut himself a nice fat cigar and, before lighting it up in the study, lifted his champagne glass. This was quite like old times.

'Rubber and oil, Baldur. Rubber and oil.'

'Quite, uncle.'

'Oh, it is no secret. We are short of them both. But we have ways of making them, believe me.'

Then, puffing his fat cigar, right out of the blue, Uncle Siegfried said, 'Tell me, Baldur. Dentz's Garnele. The contraption worked satisfactorily?' He saw Wolz's expression. He smiled. 'The very fact that you are still alive means they didn't, at least, kill you.'

'Between the Garnele and the British,' said Wolz, drily, 'they tried.'

He'd met the Herr Professor Dentz here in his uncle's schloss. His uncle was privy to many secrets. Wolz ought to feel no surprise that his uncle was aware of the Garnele, the midget submarine Dentz had developed. In one of those contraptions Wolz had penetrated the anchorage of Barca in the Med to sink British submarines, to find the coop empty and the birds flown. He'd only just returned from Africa after his experiences there. He told Uncle Siegfried a little, with an emphasis on the technical aspects. Then they drifted onto family matters.

'I have not heard from Lisl in some time,' said Wolz.

His uncle puffed his cigar. 'No? She is busy, I hear. I, myself, have not seen her for longer than I would care for. She has changed, too, you know, Baldur.'

'We all have.'

Mariza, his uncle's secretary, was away visiting his aunt. Wolz had looked forward to a romp and a bath or two with Mariza. In that, too, he was disappointed.

Jupiter and the rest of the horses were long gone, so Wolz could not take a long leisurely ride out into the countryside. He did not care to dwell on the thought of Jupiter or any of the others hauling panje wagons in Russia ... Not at all.

His uncle had been told that the army were using the horses in France, bringing up rations to the troops along the coast, and believed it. Wolz would have liked to have believed that, also.

'The social life has disappeared, Baldur, I know, around here. What will you do now?'

'Keep on pestering for a command.'

'Besides that.'

'Well, Willi Weidman and Rudi von Falkensbach are both at sea.' Wolz shook his head in a ruminative way, chewing over in his head old times spent with his comrades. 'I'd certainly like to see them again. But –'

'Precisely.'

Wolz perked up. He stared at his uncle.

'So, uncle, what exactly do you have in mind?'

'Ah!'

If what his uncle wanted him to do concerned the mousy-looking but luscious Mariza Kalman, then Wolz was all agog.

Branching off from what he had been about to say, Uncle Siegfried took a pull at his cigar and said, 'One could wish our friends the Japanese had chosen to attack the Russians rather than the Americans. I don't mind telling you, my boy, that it doesn't make a lot of sense to me.'

'I suppose they thought they were acting for the best. And they do need oil –'

'But naturally! Still, I am not engaged to worry my head over grand strategy. I have to go up to Peenemunde – new buildings or something. So I would ask you to do a little task for me.'

'With pleasure uncle. And I don't exactly envy you your trip up there at this time of the year. Although –' And here Wolz half-closed his eyes, pulling comfortably on his cigar, the champagne glass to hand on the marquetry table. 'Although it can't be as bad as the bridge of an einbaume with a seasick crew under your feet.'

'Don't talk to me of your Mark IIs – your dug out canoes. We will soon have the big new boats coming off the slips. Then, Baldur my boy, then we shall see!'

Wolz waited; but his uncle went on speaking of the task ahead. Wolz was simply required to take a briefcase to the Berlin office. It was obviously important. Uncle Siegfried would have gone himself; but he was going up to Peenemunde – what anyone in their right minds would want up there defeated Wolz – and he did not wish to entrust the papers to an underling. So – his nephew, the famous Sea Wolf, Baldur Wolz, could go and, at the same time, do the rounds of Berlin's nightspots, take in a few theatres and cinemas, perhaps visit a salon, have himself a good time on leave.

'Very good, uncle. I'm your man!'

Uncle Siegfried although able to eat well always ate with just that hint of abstemiousness that both amused and pleased Wolz. The Wolzs were not gluttons. At this time a soldier's rations on leave included allowances for about half a kilo of butter, a kilo of meat, five kilos of bread and two eggs, plus quantities of other comestibles. What was called coffee mixture – sometimes the ersatz was more sawdust than at others – was less than a quarter of a kilo, and as for real coffee – that would come in a screw of paper small enough to be blown away by a sneeze. At least the U-boatmen had real coffee. Wolz preferred the thick cocoa served in the Royal Navy they called kai; but chocolate was hard to come by. In his fortnight's rations the soldier was allowed a half a kilo of sugar and a hundred grammes of chocolate. Living in the country, living on a farm, these were big pluses. And, as the Wolzs had surmised previously, if events took the sinister course they had taken in the earlier war, then food was going to become the single overriding preoccupation of life – apart from winning the war.

'And they are still regrouping before Moscow,' said his uncle. 'I wish they'd hurry up and take the damned place.'

'I just hope that Siegfried is all right.'

'He will be, Baldur, he will be!'

'Yes.'

Berlin in wartime proved to be an incredible experience.

In some parts of the city you'd never know there was a war on. In others, and not too many, a few scars showed where British terror bombers had dropped their bombs in panic as the searchlights caught them and the flak barked up. There were queues here and there. But people were well dressed and fed, the theatres and shops and cinemas were open. The atmosphere remained still one of gaiety and lightness, perhaps not in so euphoric a strain as just after the glorious victories in France. But the music was divine, great sweeping melodies that overwhelmed the senses. And the girls!

Wolz took in the sights. His uncle had insisted on pressing a wad of Reichsmarks into his hand as the train steamed out, and short of hurling the money into the air, Wolz had to keep it. So he spent freely.

He'd always liked the cinema, although having not as many opportunities as he would have wished of seeing the latest films. There were here Tobis films and Ufa films to choose from, with the music of composers like Harald Bohmelt, Michael Jary and Theo Mackeben. As for the films, many were concoctions of froth and laughter, filled with the frisson of women's skirts, and bare shoulders, lipsticked mouths and brilliant eyes.

Wolz lapped them up.

He did wince when propaganda films were shown that were, to his professional eye, ludicrous.

Some of the pronouncements made about U-boats, for instance, would have brought his brother commanders out in cold sweats. It seemed torpedoes never missed. And as for a malfunction, that appeared to be the basest form of treachery. He could see the reason for this, of course.

But he did wonder, sitting in the darkened cinema and watching the silver ghosts on the screen, if the stories of the army and the Luftwaffe were as ridiculous. He would have to ask Manfred and Siegfried about that.

But the patrons seemed cheerful enough, lapping up whatever appeared miming and ghost-like before them.

Some of the film from Russia made you shiver, though!

He took in the show at the Metropol Theatre, and admired the shapely legs of the chorus girls.

He walked along the Wilhelmplatz, and did not fail to cast curious eyes at the buildings. Number 8/9 was Doctor Goebbels' HQ. He controlled what people saw at the cinema. He knew what he was doing, surmised Wolz, and looked at the Chancellery and the government buildings, and longed to be on the bridge of his own U-boat at sea.

There were, of course, uniforms everywhere.

When he went to the theatre to see Marlene, the auditorium was a solid sea of uniforms of every style and colour and decoration. But in the display of pulchritude no Marlene made an appearance, and when he went round to the back afterwards he was told that she was on holiday in the country and was not expected back for three weeks.

He was disappointed, and yet relieved.

He would not soon forget Marlene, nude save for her SS cap and straps, the swastika dangling between her breasts, her shiny blackboots. No, that was a memory to take to the grave.

The next day he was walking down the steps from the art gallery where he had mused over the proportions of the males and females in heroic sculpture - he was impressed by their very volume - when he bumped into Frau Heckler.

She recognised him at once.

'Herr Wolz - or, I should say, Herr Oberleutnant Wolz! How nice!'

'Frau Heckler. A great pleasure.' Wolz bowed.

She wore a black coat drawn tightly about her, so that her plumpness made her look dumpy. The coat possessed a small fur collar. Her hat was drawn down and she wore gloves. She was a round bundle from which a round cheeky pink face shone with health.

He had heard that Eric Heckler had not returned from a patrol. Heckler had belonged to the flotilla operating out of St. Nazaire and they'd lost touch after training school and periscope school. He tried to make his smile genuine.

'I was sorry about Eric -'

'Eric was a good man, and now he is dead.' She stood there, a short, plump, good-natured woman in a thin coat in the icy wind. Wolz had sent a letter, as he tried to do on these dismal occasions, feeling letters, however painful and damned difficult to write they were, were far better than the formal black-edged card that was coming so much into fashion.

'I am going to the opera with a friend,' she said, 'later on. You can buy snacks there without coupons. But –'

'Seats are not easily come by –'

'Shall I see you again, Baldur?'

People pushed past, busy about their affairs, hurrying in the chill. The steps seemed hard and grainy underfoot. Wolz suddenly realised that he'd always liked Frederika Heckler, for she was so much a part of sensible life, of caring for children, seeing to their hats and scarves and shoes, of cooking the dinner and of smiling, always smiling as he and Eric walked up the path to the open door.

'Yes,' he said. He spoke firmly. 'I should like that.'

Two days later he escorted her to the theatre.

She was living with her two children, a boy and girl of nine and seven, in a small flat in an apartment block in a part of Berlin that was respectable and yet not affluent. She did say, and he felt she spoke out of prideful despair, that she'd sent her fur coat to the collection drive for the soldiers at the Russian front. The theatre was a success, and he saw her home with great dignity. If this woman was what Germany was about, and what he was fighting for, then what he was fighting for was worth fighting for.

He saw her again a day later and then she said she could not see him the following evening for she had her shift work at the soldiers' canteen to attend to. Wolz felt a strange sense of loss on that empty evening.

A French girl came in to care for the children.

Wolz went to the cinema. When he called for Frau Frederika Heckler the next evening she was just putting on her coat. He saw that she was wearing an evening gown.

He raised his eyebrows.

She laughed, pleased at his surprise.

'Oh, Baldur, this is the evening for my regular visit to

Frau Grothe's salon. She has the most amusing people there. You'll enjoy it –'

'We-ell –'

'Now don't be a spoil-sport!'

So he went.

The house was large and sombre, in a quiet road with tree-lined pavements where sounds whispered and died. The door was opened by a round-cheeked girl in a maid's dress and apron. She took their hats and coats and then they followed the sounds of music and laughter up the curving staircase.

'This is my weekly treat, Baldur. Everyone has been so kind since Eric – since he did not come back. I expect you will meet friends – Korvettenkapitän Sammles was here last time, and Oberleutnant Kuttner.'

If he didn't meet either of those two again, Wolz wouldn't mind. But he smiled and went up the stairs at the side of this plump and pleasant woman.

He wondered if she'd missed this meeting last week. He would have felt guilty had she done so on his account.

Wolz was just thinking as they reached the top of the stairs that he would have preferred, however much he liked Frederika Heckler, some of the other women he knew to be walking upstairs with him to a party. He was consciously thinking of Lottie and Heidi, of Mitzi and Mariza, of Irmgard and Gretchen, and, running through all their faces and figures, as always, the distraught, hollow-cheeked, gaunt-eyed face of Trudi von Hartstein. He had read about extra-sensory perception. How often you thought about someone in moments before they appeared!

The door opened and a waft of music and laughter billowed out.

Riding on that wave of sound a woman stepped through. A woman dressed in a dazzling evening gown, all midnight blue with diamonds, with a low neckline and a cunning cut so that she appeared more regal than any Queen of Sheba, a woman, with pale face and brilliant eyes, walking out to the top of the steps, and staring at him, staring . . .

'Baldur!'

'Oh!' chattered Frau Heckler. 'Baldur! So you know Eva Schroder!'

10

The night passed and he was called before dawn. He went up onto the bridge of U-451 with that quick involuntary shudder leaving the fug below for the fresh nippy air. But, truth to tell, the interior of U-451 was as sweet as the armpit of a freshly-bathed girl.

For that, at least, the crew should be thankful to Fritz Gerhardt. Today they would bring him gently aboard and sink MV *Cotash* and then set about their business of sinking more enemy shipping. The convoys were not of the same calibre as the deep-water convoys crossing the Atlantic; but they offered a challenge.

With the changing of the watches, the morning watch coming down and the forenoon watch scrambling up to replace them on the bridge all in strict order and discipline, Wolz rubbed his hands. He wondered again, briefly, if he himself should go across to *Cotash*.

No.

No. That would in a sense be to indicate to Stuckl that the commander wanted to check on the IIWO's work. And that was not the case at all. The unfortunate business of the English naval officer had been handled. Because he had been expecting an incident of some kind, Wolz was not thrown off balance in his judgements. If any kind of judgement in wartime was not being hurled clean off balance.

He looked up the sheer side of the ship. U-451 rode alongside, nuzzling in, the steuermann concentrating on Wolz's quick words as he held the conn. The U-boat eased up alongside, abreast of the engine room. They'd lower Gerhardt down strapped into his stretcher without fuss, neatly and economically, and they would take the greatest care of him. Wolz knew they would. He had told them. Explicitly . . .

Before that delicate operation could take place there were other operations that must be carried out.

Stuckl knew what to do.

The Germans had behaved with perfect correctness so far in their dealings with the British, both crew and passengers. There might, now that the ugly moment had at last arrived, there might now be an explosion of fury.

If that fury burst from the British side, that would be perfectly understandable. And, if it broke out from the German side, that, too, was understandable, a part of German nature. Sometimes even the best of fellows lost their heads. Even Cousin Siegfried, normally the most correct of men, could blow all his fuses.

He'd once told Wolz of an ugly little incident, involving Reinhard Heydrich. The details were of no importance. Wolz knew that Heydrich had been a naval officer, kicked out for getting a girl into trouble and then not behaving as it was thought an officer of the Kriegsmarine should behave. Now Heydrich was a very big bug indeed in the SD, the biggest, and Siegfried, by what he did not say more than by what he did, indicated that he couldn't stand Heydrich. The detestation in Siegfried's voice when he mentioned the SD and the cronies of the bureaux involved positively dripped.

When a senior officer blew up, lesser mortals suffered.

Wolz felt he was right to trust Stuckl to keep proper order in the British ship. The lesson of Chalfont had been lost on no one, British or German. No one wanted anything like that to happen again.

The routine of the boat went along smoothly. Smutje produced meals with unfailing regularity and cheerfulness; how he did it was a mystery. Sometimes, at the end of a patrol when the decent provisions had been eaten, the bread and potatoes gone rotten, the dangling stalactites of sausages shrunken, the challenge of cooking meals became too much for a mere mortal man. But that was on the way back to base, and because of that single fact could be tolerated, if not welcomed.

And now, of course, they had all the plunder of *Cotash* to eat up . . .

In the British ship Stuckl and his men went about their task smartly, firmly and prepared to stand no nonsense.

Standing no nonsense, that was a good description of the attitude of the powers that be. Often and often Wolz had seen Cousin Siegfried crumple up his copy of the SS weekly newspaper, *Das Schwarz Korps*, hurl it into the corner of an armchair and go striding off into the garden and out into the estate, bowling along and expanding his lungs. No one was inclined to comment on his behaviour, least of all his own father.

Being a simple sailor, for Wolz, had always seemed a drawback in these high affairs; but he escaped a deal of the continual suspicion and distrust of neighbour for neighbour. He knew Stuckl, for instance, to be a good National Socialist, and not at all sorry – at least for the moment – that he had been transferred from the army into the navy. A few more patrols, a few more wabos blowing up around his neck, and Stuckl might change his tune. But, then, being blown up on the Russian Front was no picnic, either . . . So Stuckl could get on with shepherding the British into the lifeboats, and make sure they behaved.

In what he considered to be a common-sense act, Wolz had brought Torpedo Mechaniker Hans Braun back off *Cotash* to U-451 and replaced him with another hand. That seemed not only sensible but also sensitive to the feelings in the British ship.

The weather looked to be set fair. It should be a fine day.

A fine day for sending a fine ship to the bottom.

T. R. Antrobus chewed so doggedly on the stem of his bulldog that First Officer Ogilvie thought the old man would champ clean through.

'That's the way of it, mister,' said Antrobus, around the pipe. 'We lower the lifeboats and push off.'

'And then these Squareheads sink *Cotash*?'

'They do.'

This was a prospect to daunt and depress anyone.

'If only that Yank destroyer would come back –'

Antrobus switched his pipe about in his teeth. 'If he did, you know what happened last time.'

Ogilvie, thin and hollow, looked mutinous.

'We'd find a way, sir, we'd damn well find a way!'

'Well, mister, the Yank's not here. And the Jerry U-boat is. Se we do as they say. I don't want any more of my passengers machine gunned down.'

'No, sir.'

'Right, mister. Carry on.'

James Ogilvie went off to see about lowering the boats.

Even with the extra people aboard – the gunners, mostly – there were ample places in the lifeboats. The davits swung out, with a deal of flaking paint, the lines ran and tautened, the men grumped and heaved when they were told. With a whine of high-power machinery, the first of the lifeboats lowered to the sea.

Antrobus was leaning on a chart studying his best course to the east coast of America when Stuckl came into the charthouse.

'It is essential, captain,' he began in German, and then half-turned back and shouted, 'Meyer!'

Fishanchips Meyer walked in, his face wooden.

When they had that sorted out, Antrobus understood that he was to load all his people into the boats. All of them.

'But –'

'No buts, captain,' said Meyer. 'The officer means it. You must all go and row away, clear off, vamosse.'

Antrobus fumed.

But, at the least, he could see that his crew was being given a chance. If the U-boat commander had simply shot a damn great hole in *Cotash*'s side whilst everybody was aboard and then sailed off that would not have surprised him.

Leutnant z. S. Franz Stuckl made up his mind that he would exercise extra special care when he brought the British soldiers up on deck. He had a party with machine pistols aimed. The men kept their fingers on the triggers. Stuckl was not playing games.

At the slightest sign of resistance, of trouble, he'd bellow the order for his men to shoot.

The British came out onto the deck blinking in the sunlight. They brought their possessions with them, kitbags and packs, even greatcoats. They shuffled into a line along the deck. Stuckl, trim in his Kriegsmarine uniform, however bearded he might be, stood watching.

The merchant marine sailors formed up, lugging suitcases.

When the passengers appeared the steward Antrobus had told to continue to look after his charges looked run ragged. But he scuttled about in his white monkey jacket, seeing that dropped articles were retrieved, carrying cases, shouting at the couple of hands the captain had told off to help.

MV *Cotash* might only be a passenger cargo liner; but her master and her steward knew how to look after their passengers.

The boats swung, ready and open, waiting.

The Chief came on deck with a suspicious bulge down the leg of his trousers. It fell to Reinhardt Pongratz, from South Germany, to investigate the object. Pongratz jerked his MP38 as Stuckl bellowed the order. Angus Macbright stepped out to stand alone before the others. Agnes Prothero put a shaking hand to her lips, her eyes staring at Macbright, her whole body shaking.

'Whisht, man –'

Meyer, copying Stuckl, shouted, 'Put your hands up! Stand still!'

Pongratz went fishing and hauled out a six inch spanner. Macbright jumped when the end came free.

'Careful, careful, ye great Nazi ape.'

As Macbright jumped as the spanner clipped him coming out of his waistband, so Miss Prothero jumped in anguished sympathy ...

The situation needed only a tiny nudge, one way or the other. Stuckl had no monocle to grind haughtily into his eye; but he stared at Macbright. The Chief stared back, looking most evil.

The tension crackled like static electricity in the air.

Miss Prothero, knees quivering beneath the sensible dress, stepped out from the row of passengers. She looked hard at the Chief.

'Mr Macbright! When I asked to borrow a six inch spanner, I didn't mean a six inch spanner, I meant a six inch spanner.'

She held up her wood and canvas folding chair. She shook it open, and one side collapsed.

'You are kindly offered to screw up this loose nut for me –'

Fishanchips Meyer translated all this in a swift rush of German, and he spoke loudly. Stuckl's invisible monocle dropped on its black silk invisible ribbon.

The German crew of U-451 started to laugh.

The crew and passengers of MV *Cotash* started to laugh.

And T. R. Antrobus, master of the doomed vessel, felt his lips twitching. They were all laughing, out there, at an old lady's idea of a six inch spanner. But Antrobus felt the ludicrousness of it – if Miss Prothero was a loose nut, Angus Macbright was the man to screw her tight. But tight.

Laughing, the deck rang with laughter, shrill, racketting, losing control ...

Sergeant Dave Brown was not laughing.

He stood lumpily, his kitbag with the black painted canvas encircled with coloured rings, his number stencilled in white, leaning between his legs. His big pack was on his back, his haversack at his side, his respirator at the other side. No SMLE snugged between thumb and forefinger of his right hand.

And the weight of the three tapes on his arms nearly bore him down.

He was not laughing.

Standing just in front of him, a great lout of a Jerry was grinning away like the village idiot. Big, moon-faced, the Nazi bastard held his submachine gun across his guts, and his finger was not on the trigger.

Sergeant Dave Brown leaped.

He could see very little past the blaze of hatred in his head, obscuring his vision with a strange reddish halo around his eyes. His sight was narrowed to a tunnel. He got his fingers on the Schmeisser and wrenched it away. The big German reacted sluggishly.

Dave Brown swung the gun. He smashed the barrel alongside the German's face and sent him staggering back. The Schmeisser felt odd; but it was a gun, with a butt of a sort, and a barrel, a trigger. Dave Brown pulled the trigger.

The stream of 9-mm shots ripped into Peter Dorndorf's big body in the grey uniform. He staggered back, tripping over his feet, not really comprehending what was happening. He felt someone hitting him in the belly, just as his father used to hit the dog with a big ash stick, only the hits were harder and more savage. Blackness started to descend on Peter Dorndorf. He thought of the little house in the Dieterstrasse, and the wooden fence around the garden, and his little plot of that garden where he liked to grow his flowers, which he would carefully attend to when he returned from school, before even beginning his homework.

Peter Dorndorf fell down. Blood leaked from his big body.

Franz Stuckl felt icy bands clamp around his head.

He lifted his Walther P-38 and aimed it at the madman in the British battledress. The man appeared to be possessed. His face was distraught with a passion Stuckl understood only too well.

Shocked cries broke out. Men were shouting. Miss Prothero screamed and fell. Angus Macbright, bereft of his six inch spanner, leaped for her to support her.

The look on Dave Brown's face resembled very much the drawn back, teeth-exposing look on the faces of dogs as they ripped into a wild creature they had disturbed. He swung the machine pistol around –

Stuckl shot three times.

Dave Brown stopped moving.

For a moment he stood, knees half-bent, the MP38 dangling from nerveless fingers.

There was very little left of his head. Stuckl was a good shot and a finicky man.

Dave Brown collapsed.

The machine pistol was scooped up instantly by a shaking and enraged U-boatman.

'Steady!' called Stuckl. He didn't want the incident made any worse than it was. 'He's dead.'

The man who had snatched up the machine pistol, Franz Lofheimer, shook. But he did not pour a stream of bullets into the murdering Englishman. He looked up towards the officer.

'Very good!'

But, as Franz Stuckl knew, it was not at all very good.

A great babble of shouting broke out. Everybody wanted to talk at once. The U-boatmen pointed their weapons and for a few more moments it was touch and go.

A white cap appeared on the bridge of U-451.

A magnified voice reached the people shouting and waving their firsts and demonstrating on the deck of *Cotash.*

First in German, and then in English, Baldur Wolz spoke through the loud hailer.

'Silence. Stand still. Not a man moves.'

The Germans obeyed instantly.

The English took no notice.

Wolz half-turned to the men at the 2-centimetre Flak.

'Fire a half dozen shots into the air over their heads. Don't hit anyone.'

'Very good!'

The 2-cm burst into its hysterical blattering.

In the shocked silence that followed that brutal exposition of power, Wolz called across again.

'Silence. Stand still.'

He watched. Uneasily, the British stood still.

The two men lying sprawled on the deck, one in field grey, the other in khaki, with the blood running greasily, told the story.

'Herr Leutnant! Have the bodies properly attended to. Get the prisoners into the boats and get them away. Make it fast.'

T. R. Antrobus stepped forward. His bulldog rotated in his mouth, and he snatched it out and pointed at the dead sergeant.

'You can't expect us to go off and leave him –'

'We shall attend to it, captain.'

'But –'

'I do not wish to argue with you. I wish to avoid further unfortunate and unnecessary bloodshed. One of my men is dead, also.'

One master of his ship, the other commander of his U-boat, they stared at each other across the gap of water separating them. Wolz could just see enough to tell him what had occurred; had the shooting taken place away from the rail he could have seen nothing. As it was a swung-out lifeboat blocked off a deal of his view. Antrobus shook his fist.

His voice cracked in the effort to bellow across the gap with the slap and run of water past the two hulls.

'You'll pay for this, you murdering Nazi butchers –'

Stuckl appeared at Antrobus's side.

'The English soldier killed Dorndorf, Herr Kapitänleutnant, before I shot him. The fault lies with the English.'

No doubt it did. Wolz wanted the English off the ship, fast. This was exactly the kind of incident he had wished to avoid, as he had in all honesty told the British master, and it had happened. Well, he would see it did not happen again.

'Herr Leutnant! No more words. Just get them all away in the boats. As fast as you can.'

'Very good!'

'And, Herr Leutnant. Assure the master that a correct and proper burial at sea will be held for the dead Englishman.'

Wolz lowered the loudhailer. He knew that was probably not really good enough. Had he been an Englishman in that ship, with a comrade shot dead, he'd want to know the burial service had been carried out correctly, and would want to be there in person to pay his last respects. But that would make no difference to the dead man. And the smell of unrest hung in the air, raw and forbidding. If the English were not got off the ship at once, there would be more trouble.

He could feel that, strong and unmistakable.

Stuckl would be in no mood to stand any more nonsense. Wolz, again, could attach no blame to his IIWO. In this kind of undignified, tricky, complicated dealing with the enemy anything was likely to happen.

The real test was in making transactions with the enemy dignified. If that could be done, there lay hope for the future of mankind.

The boats lowered, filled with the disembarking crew and passengers.

They splashed into the sea and the oars fended them off the sheer steel sides. The motor launch containing the master started her engine, and tow lines were passed. The boats tailed on. The sea was calm. The sky was clear. The wind blew a gentle zephyr. There was no apparent problem in all the lifeboats reaching shore safely. Wolz was thankful for that. He had seen enough of men screaming in the water, men alight in a sea of burning oil, men dead and rotting in watery graves.

He waited until the launch towed the boats well clear of the ship and U-451 before giving his next series of orders. Then he went below. He changed into his full dress uniform, the full rig, medals and all. But he retained his white capcover. Then he went up onto his bridge, ready for the funeral service for two men, one British, the other German, and he knew with bitterness that he grieved for them both.

11

USS *Ackermann* secured from action stations. Lieutenant Commander Rufus K. Barnum pushed his cap back on his head and scratched his forehead. He felt no more tired than he would have been feeling had he stayed up all night playing stud. At that, there was no smoke-filled room to fray at the edges of his concentration. The day had not been entirely wasted. They had not even had so much as a solitary ping from the supposed sub; but he had exercised his crew.

'Left standard rubber. Steer course two-one-zero.'

The quartermaster piped up in a thin voice, 'Left standard rudder. Course two-one-zero.'

Barnum recognised the reedy voice of Hank Hamstein on the wheel, and realised the quartermaster hadn't gone off watch. He was a reliable man. And, anyway, he'd done no more than his skipper.

A tray bearing a cup of coffee appeared under Barnum's nose. The mess steward looked pinched around the eyes.

Ackermann continued her turn, and straightened on course home.

Barnum gave a thought to his speed, and then ordered revolutions for twenty knots. That should, given that nothing broke down in the engine room, bring them home nicely in time for everything that had to be done to be carried out without a frantic rush. He wanted to make sure his depth charge crews were on the ball, and the gun crews, and he'd have them hard at simulations all the way back. *Ackermann* was going to become a top line ship – a top line boat as the old destroyer men would say, proud of their tin cans – or Rufus K. Barnum would know the reason why.

And on this course he could probably take another look-see at the British passenger cargo liner they'd just been contacting when the sub emergency broke.

Quite probably *Ackermann*'s course and MV *Cotash*'s course would intersect.

Barnum pulled his cap back straight. Might be an idea to inquire what the signal had been about, and he made up his mind he would not mention that he had failed to locate a suspected U-boat.

Barnum saw no reason to alarm the crew of *Cotash* with reports of suspected U-boats.

The few irrational feelings Baldur Wolz experienced that he was dressing up when he put on his dress uniform for the funerals passed swiftly. Every bit of metal, every splash of colour, every ribbon on his uniform represented an act, an ideal, an oath.

The Narvik shield on his upper left arm, for instance, rather obtrusive and vulgar, denoted a very fraught time indeed with U-45 and U-55, not to mention a Tante Ju and a parachute.

The Iron Cross second class, and the First Class, also commemorated sharpish actions. If Wolz had been one of those fellows always out pot-hunting he'd be disappointed that he hadn't received a gong for knocking off three British panzers in the desert.

The weak sunshine gleamed on his white cap cover.

His square, pleasant, sharp-featured German face looked ruddy with good health and yet the pallid waxyness of the U-boatman tinged the edges with grey. Baldur Wolz, like most people, did not much care for funerals. You have to put up a brave front, think about the dead people with due reverence and, if you'd known them at all well, think more of the good times you'd had together, the fun and frolics. No good remembering a dead comrade with his insides spilling out and his face contorted in the last death scream.

Far rather think of him laughing and drinking up, of swapping jokes and chasing girls. Far rather.

Or, if the dead person happened to be a girl, then think of her laughing and full of life, beautified by her own happiness, radiant and chasing the boys. Yes, far rather …

As he had tried to think of Trudi von Hartstein …

Despite all his own savage belief in his own immortality, now he had gone through the Shadow of the Valley of Death and come through, despite that, he had had to fight very hard against the notion that Trudi was dead.

Baldur Wolz had given himself up for lost when his Bachstelze had been abandoned and his U-boat had dived leaving him abandoned in the Atlantic. But he had survived. After that he had felt that anything was possible. By rights, he should be a dead man. A ghost, mournfully haunting the sealanes where dead submariners forever shout 'Flood!' and 'Dive, dive, dive!'

And he had lived.

That miracle, it seemed, had been vouchsafed also to Trudi von Hartstein.

Eva Schroder, Frau Heckler called her.

Eva Schroder.

What was Trudi doing calling herself Eva Schroder?

He bowed like a marionette and then the radiant woman in the blue evening gown, adorned with diamonds, half-turned at the top of the stairs. She showed her profile, that profile he knew so well, and she smiled brilliantly for the man who followed her out of the room, riding on the wave of music and laughter.

Frederika Heckler touched Wolz's arm. Automatically he moved aside on the stairs.

Trudi – Eva Schroder – swung back, still laughing for the man whose arm she took, brilliant and incredibly lovely. Together they started down the stairs. Trudi shot a single swift look at Wolz, a lowering, downdrawn look of thunder, and then she was shrilling silver laughter as her escort rumbled some coarse remark concerning the habits of an acquaintance of his he had just left.

He was dressed in the full black rigout, boots, belts, jacket and breeches. His white gloves glistened. The ribbons and medals glittered. He was an SS Standartenfuhrer.

His face, animated now with the spite of his comments about the acquaintance, was coarse and bloated. Prominent veins stood out like purple worms beside his nose. His teeth were not good. Wolz hated him on the spot.

The buffoon had even gone so far as to wear his decorated *dolch*, and the SS ceremonial dagger dangled like an unwanted toothpick. He wore an aluminium wire aguillette and was probably on the staff of some high ranking SS officer.

Baldur Wolz stood, seething, as Trudi waltzed down the stairs.

'I thought,' Frau Heckler said in a breathy voice, 'I thought you knew each other?'

'Once,' said Wolz. 'A long time ago.'

A young man in a civilian suit, a pasty-faced young man with shifty eyes and slicked dark hair, sidled out of the room. He edged down the stairs, muttering an apology to Frau Heckler as he passed. He wore fancy shoes that disgusted Wolz. He went on down, and Wolz forgot him and turned to Frederika Heckler, who was looking upset.

'It is no good crying over things that are past, Frederika. You are not to have your evening spoiled.'

'Baldur – you could not spoil it for me.'

He tried his best to live up to her expectations of him; but it was hard. He kept seeing Trudi as he had first met her, young and with the moisture still damp and glittering on her butterfly wings. And then of her face and figure, distraught face, skimpy figure, in the old clothes in the wood, and the machine pistols hammering. And, now –

Now she was radiant again, supremely beautiful, dressed expensively, conscious of her power and sexual allure, on the arm of a buffoon in the black of the SS.

He tried to push Trudi von Hartstein from his mind, and failed.

Anyway, the SS oaf should have been wearing field grey.

After all, it was wartime. Or didn't this stay-at-home jackanapes, clerking in some fusty office, realise that?

Seething, Wolz realised that the sod was quite clearly successful. He was full-fleshed, brimming with confidence, secure in a safe job, able to order subordinates about, on the way up.

Well, of course, the way up carried perils, also. The SA had been put down - very properly, according to most people - only eight years ago, and then the very highest ranks had not saved their holders.

The rest of the evening passed. Of course it passed, for Wolz found himself the next morning shaving and dressing and preparing for nothing much; but where the evening had gone he had no idea.

He just hoped he had not been overly rude to Frau Heckler.

He thought he might as well go out for a morning paper. There might be some news - real news, that was.

With the paper folded under his arm he started to stroll along, not feeling the cold overmuch - the bridge of a U-boat in the North Atlantic gave one plenty of practice in the tricks of ignoring cold - and a man stepped from a shadowed shop window.

'Herr Oberleutnant Wolz?'

The first thing to notice was that the man wore a civilian coat. It was not made of black leather. He was smiling in a friendly way. Wolz peered at him. He'd seen that weak-chinned, shifty-eyed face before ...

'Herr Wolz. Would you please be so kind as to walk along with me for a space? There are things we must discuss.'

'Discuss?'

Then, 'You were on the stairs -'

'Precisely.'

Wolz had enough presence of mind not to bring up the subject uppermost in his head. People could be stopped and asked questions and then be taken away. If you were not a good National Socialist you must live in fear of some unknown happening. Being a sailor had removed Wolz from almost all that horror. So he did not mention the Gestapo.

They walked along, and any observer would have thought them merely out for a morning stroll. The naval leutnant on leave and a friend, probably a ministry official.

'In here.'

Here was a black auto – not a Mercedes. Wolz got in.

Trudi von Hartstein leaned over and kissed him.

Her lips pressed against his. They felt soft and moist, hot, half-parted. She gripped him with her left arm. He felt her fingers digging into his back through the heavy naval greatcoat, and then he could feel only the softness of her pressed against him, the softness of her lips.

Dizzied, he drew back and, instantly, she lifted her gloved right hand and pressed three fingers against his mouth.

'Drive on.'

The car started.

'Baldur – Baldur – you should not have seen me. Not again.'

Then she lifted those three fingers and said, 'As Eva Schroder, please, Baldur.'

He said, 'Not Karin, then?'

Her perfume clung in his nostrils, subtle and disturbing. He had hungered for this girl and now she was a woman. He'd been disturbed by her temptation, her offer, when she'd called herself Karin, to give him a night of love so that he would do her will and drive her to the Bodensee. He'd taken her down to the border, and he had not touched her, save to kiss her as she collapsed all naked against him.

And, now, again –

'What do you want me to do for you this time?'

She looked steadily at him, and the warmth of the car interior worked on Baldur Wolz, muffled in his heavy greatcoat. She wore a pencil-slim skirt and jacket, in a patterned grey, and her face looked the face of an angel in hell.

She touched the jacket where it opened to reveal a white blouse.

'I shall not offer you myself – again, Baldur.'

'Not Wolfgang, then, this time?'

Her eyebrows drew down and together. Wolz could see she was puzzled by his attitude. He could not fully understand himself, either. He felt hurt.

'I told you I had planned to ask you to marry me, twice. Each time –'

'You helped me –'

'And when you offered your bribe –' He put out a hand and stripped off the glove. Then, gently, he put his fingers under her chin, tilted her head. By God! But she was lovely!

'When you undid those silly black buttons, all in a row on the grey dress –'

'Yes?'

Carefully, he moved his hand down from her chin, twitched the jacket aside. Her blouse moved as she breathed. He put his hand on her right breast, held it there, feeling the roundness and heaviness. Her face remained pale, absorbed. She regarded him with a deep concentration – or could it be compassion.

'Do you love me, Baldur?'

She did not know, he thought, of Cousin Lisl.

'Yes.'

He took his hand away.

'There is a piece of paper – it must reach a certain person – and an address – and that is all.'

'That is all.'

Her head went back.

'You mock me, Baldur. But I assure you, I assure you with everything in me, that I do nothing to harm Germany. Do you believe me?'

'I believe you mean what you say.'

'That is not good enough.' She half-turned away from him on the upholstered seat and drew down the blind separating the driving from the passenger compartment. She turned back. She was breathing faster. 'I asked you if you loved me and you said yes. You did not ask if I loved you.'

He shook his head. 'I did not need to ask –'

'No? Why?'

'Because, clearly, you do not.'

'Baldur –!'

'Where is this famous piece of paper? What is it, a death list for the Gestapo?'

'Don't joke –'

'I am not joking. Only a fool jokes about the Gestapo, or the SD, or Sipo or Kripo or any of them –'

'I agree. It is not a death list. It is a list that will save lives.'

He looked hard at her, suddenly realising . . .

'Jewish lives?'

'No.'

A silence fell. She pulled the other side of her jacket back and the white blouse moved. Wolz felt hot and uncomfortable in the greatcoat. Then –

'Would it have made a difference had they been Jewish lives?'

He could answer that in honesty. 'I do not know.'

She began to undo the buttons of the blouse.

Because Baldur Wolz had often and often kicked himself in the long watches, standing braced on the bridge of a U-boat, suffering the vile conditions submariners operated under, kicking himself mentally for not taking Trudi when he had had the chance, he leaned back. He watched her. She was completely composed.

The blouse opened. She reached in and, somehow, the chemise was no longer in the way.

'I would like you to take the piece of paper to a Herr Adolf Braun. I will give you the address.'

Now her slender hands vanished from view behind herself. She leaned forward and her breasts trembled in the cups of the brassiere. Wolz licked his lips.

The car lurched.

It skidded around a corner and Wolz glanced swiftly through the side window.

He did not know whereabouts in Berlin they might be. Grey houses passed in a blur. There were very few people about. It was going to snow very soon. The car turned another corner, and Wolz looked back.

Around a corner a following car skidded and then straightened up. It accelerated after them.

The car was black, not a Mercedes, and it looked in a way horrifying to Wolz, dark and sinister.

He looked back to Trudi.

The brassiere had fallen away on one side, the left side, and her breast showed, white with faint blue veins. The nipple was hard and red and erect. She held herself absolutely still, looking out the back window.

Then she pushed her breast back, pulled the brassiere up and reaching back, clipped it in place.

'Not now, Baldur. Business before pleasure.'

'What –'

'Joa – the driver is very good. But, just in case he cannot throw them off . . .'

Her handbag was large, of leather, fastened by a gilt clip. She opened the bag, rummaged about and then lifted out a Walther P38.

Wolz looked on in horror.

'You're walking about Berlin with that in your handbag! Are you crazy!'

'Only sometimes.'

Wolz snapped his mouth shut. He took a breath.

'Is that car full of policemen, Gestapo –?'

'I do not know. I do know one thing. It is full of murdering butchers. They will kill me if they catch me. After they have tortured me and had fun with me – those that aren't queers, that is.'

And Wolz, dimly, heard himself say, 'They'll have their fun with you, my girl, don't you fret.'

'So I believe.'

No thought was necessary.

He did not believe Trudi could be involved in any criminal activity. She was not working against Germany. What she was doing was dangerous; but if she was captured by the thugs of the SS – people very far removed from Cousin Siegfried, people Cousin Siegfried detested with the virulence of an idealist who sees scum besmirching his ideals – then she was doomed.

'Can you shoot that thing?'

'Oh, yes.'

'That buffoon of an SS Standartenfuhrer you were with last night. Is he in that car?'

She flicked her gaze at him before turning to look back at the pursuing car.

'Heini? He operates a sonderkommando specialising in the bastinado. You know what that is?'

'Yes.'

'If he just happened to be in that car, and I saw him, I'd probably shoot straighter.'

'Has he slept with you?'

'No. He thinks he will; but I'll cut him off in his prime first.'

The car lurched again and the thin scream of overstressed tyres raked up. The pursuing car took the corner more heavily, skidding before recovering. They were rushing through a poor part of the city, where mean hovels crowded. There were a few bomb sites here, not many, and Wolz surmised there would be railway lines nearby.

They hurtled across a wider road, and for a fleeting moment, seeing the trams, Wolz thought it must be the Pfortzenheimstrasse. But he wasn't sure, and the car bore him on, Trudi clutching the big automatic, and hurled him into a network of grimy streets.

She leaned forward and lifted the curtain.

'Joachim! Take the second left – you know, past the bridge.'

'Very good!'

Seedy-looking he might be, but this Joachim could drive.

The car fairly flew around the corner. Joachim wrestled the wheel. A brick wall reared at them, and they skidded past with a spiderweb to spare.

The pursuing car failed to make the turn.

Glaring back in appalled fascination, Wolz saw the car smash straight into the wall. The car reared. It hurtled up, toppling end over end. When it hit the explosion was something like an eel hitting a ten thousand ton tanker.

He shut his eyes.

'Stop the car,' Trudi was saying.

Wolz's eyelids flew up.

'Stop the car? Are you mad? They'll –'

'Quiet, Baldur, *please.* I have some experience in these things.'

The car stopped and Trudi, both gloves on, stepped out. The driver slammed his door. Wolz climbed out and shivered with the bitter cold.

No one appeared to be giving them any attention. The explosion, three streets away, and the rising column of black smoke, drew all attention. Trudi began to walk away. She carried her wide brimmed hat in her hand, and it covered the automatic. A few steps away, at the corner, she turned.

'Move on, you two. This will only take a minute.'

Wolz went on and then stopped.

Trudi lifted the Walther P38, shot it into the car's petrol tank. Just which shot ignited the accumulation of vapour in the top of the tank, Wolz didn't bother to count.

All he knew was that there was another damned tanker blowing up, and he was grabbing Trudi's arm and forcing her to run. He heard Joachim's footsteps at his back, and then a hard object jammed in between his ribs.

'Stop running, my friend. Now. Or I shall shoot.'

Wolz stopped running.

He was breathing in gasps, and the vapour blew out in white jets like a steam train impatient at a halt signal.

'You idiot! Joachim is quite right!'

She was outraged. Two red spots flamed in her cheeks.

She drew her coat about herself, pulling it forward from its perch around her shoulders. Her gun had vanished. Joachim helped her get her arms into the sleeves of the coat. Then the three of them began to walk gently along, turning into another road and, crossing it, emerging into a part of the city where Wolz felt respectable people who would have nothing to do with guns and burning cars lived orderly lives.

Well, as orderly as anyone could live a life in wartime Germany.

'I need a coffee – or brown sawdust water,' she said. 'Here, here is the paper. Now take it, ask no questions, and perhaps, if we are lucky, we shall see each other again.'

This wasn't good enough for Baldur Wolz.

'Look, Tr – Eva! You can't–'

'I can. I have to.' She spoke to the driver. 'Joachim. Go and call.'

'Yes, Eva.'

When he'd walked off towards a shop on the same side, Wolz and Trudi continued to stroll along together. Wolz felt like running; but he knew Trudi spoke sweet truth. He felt hot and cold, the sight of her with her blouse undone and her brassiere – and then the following car and the explosion. No thoughts of going back to help had occurred to him. They were too damn late now, that was for sure.

'Would you still ask me to marry you?'

'Yes.'

'Despite all – all this?'

'Yes.'

'And you will deliver the paper? You will be careful?'

'Who should I be careful of?' He spoke hurtfully.

The pressure of her gloved fingers on his arm increased. 'The men in that car would be killed, I'm sure of it –'

'So am I.'

'– so they're all right. You have a presence and a position. But – there are many men in concentration camps, and women and children as well – and what happens is horrible –'

'They have to work –'

'Oh, Baldur! You're just besotted with propaganda! They kill people there –'

'I can't believe that. The Führer wouldn't allow it.'

'The Führer!'

He felt bewildered, and, also, scared.

'If the truth ever gets out, Baldur, and one day it will, believe me, then you'll see what a fool you and all those like you are.' She was panting. 'But forget about me, now.'

'I can't.'

'Just deliver the paper, and go back to sea. You'll be perfectly safe.'

'Perfectly safe – at sea in a U-boat?' And Baldur Wolz laughed.

A long black shiny car drew up beside them. It was a Mercedes this time, with a swastika flag, and Trudi entered and slammed the door and drove away, and Baldur Wolz was left on the pavement alone with his empty laughter . . .

12

The burials at sea of Sergeant Dave Brown, Royal Artillery, and Gefreiter Peter Dorndorf, Torpedo Mechaniker, Kriegsmarine, were completed.

Kapitänleutnant Baldur Wolz read the service, first in English and then in German. The two bodies slid from under the flags, from beneath the Union Jack and the Nazi flag, plunging down like two arrows seeking the mysteries beyond the grave.

The splashes opening in white rings of foam looked woefully small in all that expanse of ocean.

Pipes shrilled, whistles the British called them sometimes, to Wolz's amusement, and the hands were stood down. What a mysterious and messy business death amidst life was!

The very superficiality of that reaction to a profound and moving experience made Wolz realise afresh how blunting to the sensibilities war was. How easy to mouth the expected platitudes. But two men were dead. Their lives would make no, or practically no difference to their deaths, and their deaths would not affect the war. But, still and all, maybe their lives had had something to do with their deaths, after all . . .

Something must have been driving that maniacal Englishman, quite apart from patriotism.

Something had been driving Trudi von Hartstein, and she had passionately avowed that it was patriotism in its purest form.

Wolz wanted to believe her. He knew now, quite without any hypocrisy, that he wanted her. The sight of her in the back of the car, as the brassiere fell free, had been a different experience from that earlier flaunting of her sexual beauty and allure. She was honest about herself, that struck through to Wolz.

He'd delivered the paper to Herr Adolf Braun, and some meek little man in pince nez, with the lapel button and the spats, had snuffed and sniffled and taken it into the hotel. Wolz left immediately. Later a telephone call filled in a little more of the details. Trudi had spoken guardedly.

'No one saw you, Baldur, no one at all. Apart from those no longer with us.' And, then, 'It was the vehicle that aroused interest, the car that was being followed. I was remiss in that.'

He surmised, and as he was still at liberty he must be correct in the assumption, that the telephone conversation was not being monitored, and that Trudi knew that. All the same, she was as enigmatic as ever.

'I've been given orders,' he told her. He did not tell her that he'd been ordered to Brest. What they wanted to send him to Brest for he had no idea. He'd asked for a U-boat command, and with the flotilla at Lorient, and they were sending him to Brest. The omens were not good.

'Perhaps we shall never meet again,' she said. He could hear her breathing. 'Take care, Baldur.'

'And you – if you can –'

'I can still feel –'

'I meant what I said –'

'I hope so. I can still feel your touch on my skin – I felt – I felt as though you'd touched me with an electric current. Is that foolish?'

'No. The soles of my feet are still tingling.'

She laughed. That was the first laugh he'd heard from her in a long long time – a true laugh.

'We'll electric current and tingle again, you'll see.'

'We will!'

But, as he stared down at the rapidly disappearing rings of foam and ripples where two men had finished with this world, he wondered heavily if they had been merely whistling in the wind, Trudi von Hartstein and Baldur Wolz. Just two little fools caught up in the whirlwind of events.

And he would not, could not, think of Cousin Lisl ...

Far better, when he was not dreaming of Trudi, to reflect on Heidi or Lottie, and to recall the romps with Gretchen and Irmgard. Far better.

Thoughts like that, despite the frustrations they engendered, kept at bay the madness that afflicted U-boatmen in the cold wastes of the sea.

'Herr Leutnant Stuckl!'

'Commander?'

Wolz nodded. 'Get the hands on shipping the loot across.' Commander and Kapitän were interchangeable terms, in his book, and provided they called him skipper to his face and Daddy among themselves, he'd be satisfied. 'We'll bring Fritz off last. And, Franz, we'll take care with the old rascal.'

'We will, skipper. He's feeling much better now, thanks be.'

'Good!'

U-451 nuzzled alongside MV *Cotash.* Her paint blended with the flaked side of the ship. Wolz took a look around, aware with that towering wall of steel at his side of the low vantage point of a U-boat's conning tower. His bridge lofted just above the waves. The ship rose from the water, solid, bold, dominating. Well, an eel into that imposing steel flank would sink the old darling, sink her to the bottom of the sea.

Not good, said Wolz to himself, and went below.

The hands would be swarming through *Cotash* now, stripping out anything they took a fancy to. He wouldn't stop that. Better it should grace the locker or the pockets of an honest German *matrose* than moulder in the slime of the sea bed.

He had just opened the log at the page to begin recording the melancholy details of the burials at sea when the explosion shocked through the boat.

U-451 lurched and jumped. She shuddered.

Instinctively, Wolz knew his command had been struck a mortal blow.

Shouts racketted through the boat.

He was out of the wardroom, into the *zentrale*, bellowing.

'Still!'

The hands obeyed. The boat was down by the head.

The cox'n checked with the forward torpedo room, and turned a haggard face towards Wolz.

'No answer!'

'Up with you,' said Wolz. 'All of you. Up onto the English ship.'

It was the first idea that occurred to him.

By her movements he knew U-451 was going down by the head. Like an arrow, she would join those two other arrows that had burrowed deep into the water.

He was still clutching the log, still dressed in full fig, medals and decorations, the lot. No time to think of that now. The men stumbled up the metal rungs of the ladders, their feet loud, shouting, pushing. But discipline did not break. U-451 tilted further by the head.

The cox'n reported that the men from the forward flats had been detailed for work in the ship, and of the others, only two were unaccounted for. By now they must be dead.

Had the forward torpedo room been filled with men, overcrowded and stuffy, with men jammed in on top of the torpedoes, those that were left, the explosion would have accounted for all of them.

As it was, the torpedo that had struck his command had killed two men at the outset.

How many more would be killed before the American or British ship made them prisoners, he did not know. He would do all in his power to make that number as small as possible.

Although, as he stared around his familiar control room, although if a destroyer had discovered them, stealing up without being sighted, why had she loosed a torpedo? And how could a destroyer approach without the lookouts seeing her? And why an eel? Why not her guns?

No time to puzzle over that now.

Time only to hug the log to him, to snatch up a few prized possessions, and to make sure no one was left aboard.

At that, he only just made it.

U-451 was diving – for the last time.

He remembered with anguished vividness the moments he had spent in the zentrale of U-55 when she'd been torpedoed in the Mediterranean. He'd been supremely confident then that he would rise clear, sucking oxygen from his Drager Escape Apparatus. He'd lost good men, and he'd saved good men. But now, once again, his command had been lost.

This time there was no need to wear escape equipment. He did not have to float up in pitch darkness and claw his way up out of his own bridge. Now he looked up into the sunlight up to the steel side of the English ship and saw the row of heads all lining the rail. Lines tailed down.

Up went the log dangling in its canvas bag.

He grabbed a line and wrapped it about himself, around his waist, over his shoulder, around again. He reached up a hand and gripped the rope. He looked up.

'Hoist away!'

Up went the commander of U-451, up, swinging on the line, feet bashing at the steel flank of *Cotash*, up and over the rail, and he was not the commander of U-451 any more, for there was no U-451 afloat, only a mangled wreck sinking deep into the sea.

The cox'n had reported two men lost and Wolz as he swung up and over the rail desperately wanted to know who those two men were – or had been.

Hands grabbed him and eased him to the deck.

He unwrapped the line and flung it away. He stared over the side, turning his back on the men clustered on the deck. Bubbles were breaking and bursting. The water churned. He thought he glimpsed a dark shark outline, beneath the surface, a slender steel shark that was gone – and then only the water, boiling and bubbling and mocking with its emptiness.

'Very good!' He swung back to his men. His face showed all the hardness built in him over these war years. 'Very good! We have lost one ship so we now have another.'

Piles of loot lay on the deck. Crates of food, crates of bottles – he would shoot anyone who tried to evade his orders about alcohol – all the precious material that would make life bearable in a U-boat just clumped there, forlorn.

'But –!' said Stuckl.

'U-boat!' The voice screeched high, almost cracking in excitement. Everyone stared eagerly out to sea.

She was there, all right.

A swirl of white water, and the periscope standards thrusting up, then the dark outline of the conning tower. The rails of the wintergarden showed spidery lines. She was a U-boat, no doubt of it, not an American or British submarine.

And then the awful realisation hit Baldur Wolz.

Water spouted out from the U-boat. A white cap cover appeared atop her conning tower. Men ran down to the 8.8-cm deck gun and cast it loose. It began to swing and the long barrel foreshortened.

If those idiots over there shot!

No doubt, Wolz surmised savagely, no doubt the cretinous U-boat commander was wondering why, when his eel had struck and caused so splendid an explosion, the British ship was not sinking.

Wolz, of U-451, could tell him.

'Find a signalling lamp,' growled Wolz. He glared balefully at the boat. She wore no number in wartime. He wondered who commanded her. Some infamous idiot, without a doubt.

The signalman ran up – if the lamp was the same one that had fallen from the dead hands of Lieutenant Commander Chalfont, Wolz did not know, or care.

'Send, "U-boat from Wolz, U-451. You have sunk my boat. Congratulations." '

The signal lamp began to clack.

The answering wink of light came swiftly. The signalman on the bridge over there would recognise a Kriegsmarine hand when he saw it.

'Wolz, U-451, from Freiwald, U-580. Repeat.'

Wolz kept his temper.

'Do as he requests, signalman.'

'Very good!'

The lamp clacked again.

There was an outside chance of an excuse for the idiot in U-580. Wolz knew who it was, if it was the same foolhardy Freiwald. U-451 had been nuzzled in alongside *Cotash*, true, a low dark streak against the ship's plating. She would not have been easy to see, true. But, for all that, a U-boat skipper ought to have spotted a fellow U-boat, surely?

There was no excuse. If this Freiwald was the same Kapitänleutnant Erich Freiwald under whose insufferable command Wolz had served for a thankfully short time in the Mediterranean, then there would be no excuse, no damn excuse at all.

He realised he was breathing deeply, dragging the air into his lungs. He was gripping the ship's rail. He was trembling.

Damn Freiwald!

The answer flickered back.

'Come aboard to discuss the situation.'

'So,' said Stuckl, on a grunt. 'He now believes he has sunk a German U-boat.'

'Can you find a ship's boat left, Franz?'

'The English left their little cockboat –'

'Right. We'll use that. I'm going across.'

'Very good.'

The lookout shouted. 'Smoke!' And then, moments later, 'A destroyer –' Wolz, everybody, stared aloft. 'American destroyer. On intercept course –'

'Send,' Wolz said to the signalman. 'Send, "American

destroyer approaching on bearing oh-three-oh." '

The lamp clicked out the signal.

Almost before the signal lamp fell silent and with no answering wink of light from the U-boat, the bridge cleared and water spouted up all along her sides. She was diving.

'Well,' grunted Wolz. 'You can't fault the idiot for that. If he gets it right this time.'

If Erich Freiwald had the sense to hang just by *Cotash*, screened from underwater detection by the big hull, and then sent his eels slap bang into the Yankee, as Wolz had planned to do, that might redress the balance.

It might make some German admirals happy.

It wouldn't recompense Baldur Wolz, though ...

The enormity of what had just happened, the tragedy, the stupid criminal waste, began to work on him. He had kept his head. He had kept calm. Two men were dead and his command sunk; and he was still able to carry on. He was still able to give orders, and maintain a grave and commanding face, still function, when he wanted to smash his fist, again and again, into the face and guts of that incompetent murdering bastard over there ...

Deliberately, he took out his silver case and extracted, for extraction was the right word now, one of his uncle's cigars. There would be many cigars in *Cotash*. But these were good Dutch cigars - not the finest but undeniably powerful - long, thin, black and devilishly ugly. He stuck the thing in the corner of his mouth. It jutted up arrogantly. He walked across the deck and his men fell back to give him space.

This was how the U-boatmen of every boat Baldur Wolz had commanded would remember him.

His cap with the white cap cover tilted just a tiny fraction, his head up and chin jutting, his blond hair slicked and gleaming beneath the cap, his blue eyes like - his blue eyes like the blue cold eyes of Baldur Wolz - he stalked among his crew like the savage animal he was. And the evil black cigar thrust arrogantly up from the corner of his lips.

'Attention! You are now British sailors. Get clothes from

slops. Get rid of anything with German insignia. And most of you keep out of sight.'

He bent a ferocious eye on Fahnrich Josef Steidle. The young man's fair hair and blue eyes were no problem; but his pudge of a nose might prove awkward. Still, maybe the Americans liked pudgy noses . . .

'Josef – find the cabin of that lady – Miss Prothero, I believe her name was. Dress up in some women's clothes.' Steidle's face looked flabbergasted. Wolz glared at him unmercifully. 'And stuff some crumpled up newspapers, or towels, up your shirt. She was an old biddy; but you know what they say about old fiddles.'

Wolz, with his keen eye, had not failed to observe, even in those disastrous moments, that Miss Prothero was endowed by nature with a beautiful bounty.

'But – skipper –'

The cigar rolled one way and rolled back.

A person with high-flown ideas of psychology might regard that cigar of Baldur Wolz's as a phallic symbol. They would be wrong. That evil black cigar was, if anything, the symbol for his trade. That cigar was, in psychological terms, the torpedo he wanted to spit out into the guts of enemy ships.

Mind you, the phallic symbol idea did have some merit, referring in particular to Baldur Wolz's other great interest . . .

Fahnrich Josef Steidle blushed. He really did.

Some of the hands thought this a highly amusing situation; but Wolz soon disabused them of that idea. As he stalked up towards the bridge the hands vanished, and presently they re-appeared with unmarked seamen's clothing.

On the bridge, with his watch about him, Wolz removed his cap.

'Fetch me a uniform from the captain's cabin – if he left any. A hat, something.'

'Very good!'

He walked out onto the bridge wing.

The Yankee was now clearly in sight. She was foaming along, shedding twin white wings. Her bow looked hard and sharp, horribly sharp. She could cut clean through a U-boat.

He looked aft. Josef Steidle was just walking along the deck, striding out in a long skirt.

Wolz bawled offensively.

'Walk like a woman, you idiot! Swing your hips! Take short steps! Don't you know how women are made?'

Steidle jumped at the blast of sound. But he shortened his steps, and minced. Wolz let his thin lips widen. He had learned from the cox'n that he could not ask the other midshipman to take the part of a woman.

Fahnrich Ulrich Rudhart was one of the two men who had been mangled and crushed by the explosion of a German torpedo. The other man was Hans Mulheim, an excellent fellow from Bonn. Well, one problem had been settled, if two more had been raised ...

The destroyer was aiming to sweep around past the bows. Wolz watched her keenly.

A light winked from her superstructure.

'What ship?'

'Hand me the lamp.' Wolz hefted the signalling lamp, got it settled comfortably, aimed it, and sent the two dashes and the opening of Beethoven's Fifth. Then, without a pause, he sent *Angmering*. That was the name of a place he and Dick Mitchell and the girls had spent a pleasant day's picnic.

'Are you in trouble?'

Of course. *Cotash* was barely moving through the water. If this fellow asked about the missing lifeboats ...

Wolz sent, 'No. Engine trouble rectified.'

He trusted the lack of code words would be accounted for by one ship being British and the other American. No doubt they'd organise codings soon enough, if they had not already. But there was nothing he could to about that. International code would have to suffice.

Then, thinking, he sent, 'Thank you for asking.'

'You signalled beware U-boat. Query?'

So that poor dead idiot had got off some blinks from his lamp.

Calmly, Wolz triggered out, 'No U-boats here.'

Well, that was only half a lie. There were no *decent* U-boats around . . .

He eyed the destroyer. She was clearly swinging around and about to alter course. He needed only a few more moments of conversation to hold her in check, and then Freiwald could slip in a couple of eels.

Wolz had no idea where U-580 was lurking. He knew where he'd be, if he was in command. At any moment, as soon as the destroyer had committed herself to her change of course, he'd feed that last reading into the attack table, then he'd bellow, *'Loose!'* and the eel would loose and the pressure air would hiss, and there would be a nice big bang.

And the Yanks would be down one nice shiny destroyer.

Willi Schneider appeared on the bridge bearing a coat so ancient its blue was grey and its gold rings a dingy ochre. He held a blue peaked cap in his other hand. The cap was small and dingy, and the black peak was practically invisible. It would come down just between the eyebrows, and would probably push the cap back, so sharply was it angled.

'Here, skipper –'

Wolz, one eye on the destroyer and calculating when she would turn and when Freiwald should loose, glanced at these dismal garments with disfavour.

'No need, Schneider, thank you. The Yankee swallowed me whole.'

'And the old lady,' said Schneider, showing his teeth, daringly, to his skipper.

The trouble about clothes was, Wolz knew he couldn't go rampaging about in full fig all the time. He'd damn well wear the lot to see that idiot Freiwald. That would add emphasis to the things he intended to say.

'I hope the old lady had the sense to hang on the rail and gawp at the Yankee.'

'Yes, skipper. The Fahnrich acted very well.'

'Good.'

Very soon Wolz could don his uniform again. As it was, he took another long look at the destroyer. She was turning. She leaned over, hard and sharp as American destroyers did with all their top hamper. Then she started to straighten out on her new course. She was aiming to make a loop about *Cotash* which she thought was *Angmering*.

Now was the moment – and then – and then!

Through the binoculars Wolz saw a faint white streak vanishing away to the distant horizon. It was thin and barely noticeable. It passed metres astern of the Yankee.

And the American destroyer straightened on her course and sailed splendidly down on the other side of *Cotash*.

Wolz snatched the glasses from his eyes.

He didn't believe it.

Freiwald had missed!

Missed a sitting duck!

The infernal incompetent murdering imbecile!

And the Yankee sailed grandly on. Wolz was prepared to bet a year's pay no one in the destroyer had spotted that faint tell tale trail. The eel was running shallow, and even an electric would leave some wake . . . It shouldn't do so; but it had, as often happened, and the Yank had been blind.

Come on Freiwald, you idiot, he said to himself. Loose again!

The destroyer was winking again.

'Goodbye and good luck.'

Forcing himself, Wolz clacked back, 'Thank you.' Then, guessing it was expected, and aware of dark and turbulent thoughts quite foreign to his nature, he sent, 'Good hunting.'

He was thinking of U-580, and already aware of the criminal irresponsibility of his thoughts.

All the same . . .

When he got aboard U-580 and used the Enigma to signal BdU, Kerneval would have something to say about this fiasco. What Dönitz would say, how he would react, to one of his U-boats being sunk by another, Wolz relished with some vindictive glee. Freiwald deserved all he got.

The destroyer steamed away, en route for home.

Wolz stared after her balefully.

He did not know her commander. He fancied he would not mind encountering him again. It was so much easier fighting a blind man.

When the destroyer had gone and the sea was empty of all save *Cotash*, U-580 surfaced and joined the ship.

The light blinked.

'All torpedoes expended. Milch cow due at rendezvous 0800 tomorrow.'

So that explained the single torpedo; it did not explain Freiwald's atrocious shooting. Any U-boat skipper worth his salt would have spotted the destroyer's change of course and adjusted his sights. Any U-boat skipper ...

Atrocious shooting was a bugbear of commanders forced to take sights through little round peepholes, making quick stabs at a look-see, able to encompass so little of the surface. Wolz had missed himself, on occasion. But, all the same ...

He supposed he could excuse Freiwald for missing. For missing even so close a target as the Yankee destroyer there could be an excuse. But Wolz was far from any frame of mind that would find an excuse for the sinking of his own command. U-451 had been sunk by a criminal imbecile.

Then the odd stray thought occurred to him that there might be a problem over survivor's leave. It would be interesting to find out. His last survivor's leave had been extraordinarily fraught, and after that contretemps with Trudi von Hartstein, calling herself Eva Schroder, in the car, he had not finished with her. Very far from it.

The surprise that awaited him when he reported himself in at the naval base of Brest still remained vividly in his mind. He pulled his coat straight and gave a twitch to his cap. The white cap cover gleamed. His slicked blond hair gleamed. The decorations on his uniform gleamed. And his teeth glinted evilly around the evil black cigar.

He'd go across to see Kapitänleutnant Eric Freiwald and let him know what kind of all-fired fool he was.

After that they'd rendezvous with the milch cow and sink *Cotash* and go back to base.

And, after that - another U-boat?

Probably.

A great deal remained to be done before the U-boat arm of the Kriegsmarine had won the war at sea. A great deal remained to be done before he understood Trudi von Hartstein and brought their unnerving relationship to a satisfying situation.

Baldur Wolz, one of the Grey Wolves, Sea Wolf, would be involved in both activities up to the hilt.

That was what they called destiny.